ADELA SAVES THE SPACE STATION

HOW AN 11-YEAR OLD RESCUED IT FROM TOTAL DESTRUCTION

MATTHEW THOMAS

ISBN-13: 978-1983788529
ISBN-10: 198378852X

DEDICATION

For Jessica S and her esteemed fellow librarians, Elva R with her wonderful bookstore, Carrie for her psychological insight, and most of all my ever-optimistic mom. Without your support, encouragement, criticism, and inspiration, this never could have happened.

CONTENTS

ACKNOWLEDGMENTS

Thank you NASA for your incredible work, firing our imagination, making our dreams real. For enabling people like Sonny White and others to try and further understand our Universe by experimenting with "physics-defying" ideas such as the Electromagnetic Drive. How small would our horizons be if we never tried to walk on the moon?

1 LAUNCH!

"ALL SYSTEMS GO," boomed the loudspeakers across the wide concrete expanse of Space Launch Complex 36 at Cape Canaveral, Florida. "READY FOR LAUNCH."

Inside Mission Control, the NASA engineers nervously double-checked their sensor readouts and launch procedures. This was the first test of their most Top-Secret project. But it was happening much sooner than planned. The President himself had ordered it. Someone had to respond to the emergency on board the international space station, and fast. NASA had the only space vehicle available.

"3, 2, 1, lift-off!" The special docking clamps released Project X, NASA's last and final hope, from the launch pad. But it did not head straight up to the international space station as planned – it almost immediately veered off course and escaped!

The National Aeronautics and Space Administration (NASA) landed the first people on the moon in July 1969, beginning with Apollo 11. Between 1969 and 1972 NASA sent 6 successful missions to the moon, each having 3 astronauts. Each mission left one person, a pilot, in the command module orbiting the moon. So, a total of 12 astronauts descended from their command module to explore the lunar surface.

These 12 Americans are the only humans to ever set foot on the moon. All returned safely to Earth, a truly incredible feat. No one has visited the moon since because it is simply too expensive, and too hard to do safely. The entire country pulled together to make this happen, a point of tremendous national pride at the time. In 1969, huge banners in small towns and factories across America proudly proclaimed their contribution to the Men Who Walked On The Moon.

NASA has sent sophisticated satellites to comets, asteroids, and all 8 planets of our solar system, giving humanity their first up-close look at alien worlds. They propelled the first probe outside the solar system, into true interstellar space, Voyager 1, where we learned deep space is very different than expected. NASA launches most of their big rockets from the Kennedy Space Center, located on Cape Canaveral, Florida.

In recent years, NASA has contracted more and more routine space launch capability, such as ferrying supplies to the international space station, to companies such as Blue Horizons and SpaceX. But there is little profit to be made for research that will not bear fruit for 20 years. NASA is the one who pays for, and continues to pay for, almost all of the advanced research needed that will someday enable humanity to make other worlds our new home.

2 NASA AND THE ALLIGATOR

Half-way across the state, Adela and Louie had finished gathering the day's eggs. It was a lazy weekend, and they were taking a break from Florida's early summer heat. Hidden in the breezy shade of Adela's tree house, they were watching the flock of wild ducks play on the lake below. Their tree house was perched high in an ancient live oak, with a commanding view of the sky above and lake below.

Adela's father started building the tree house, but she finished it herself. Tanned and strong from a life of hard farm work, she kept her brown hair cut short. Her favorite work clothes were her blue overalls because they had the most pockets (twelve), meaning the most treats for her animals. Adela kept about sixty organic milk cows content, an ever-changing number of free-range chickens fed, and her father's tractors and combines running smoothly. Her family's farm, and especially its animals, were her life.

The 160-acre farm in north central Florida had been in her father's family since 1899. Parts were never logged, with a few of the oak trees mature before the Conquistadors arrived. Its woods were filled with towering pines and huge sprawling live oaks draped in Spanish moss, interspersed with meandering grassy meadows for the rambling cows. Most fields were planted with hay, alfalfa, grain, and organic vegetables, depending on the time of year. An artesian spring supplied a small lake that was home to perch and largemouth bass, which in turn usually fed a flock of wild ducks.

Adela had no brother or sister. But she did have Louie, her extraordinarily intelligent cat and general co-conspirator, who tried his best to fill the gap. Louie was a big, strong, black and white tuxedo cat, a one-time stray kitten who chose to adopt Adela as his human. He helped Adela whenever he could, but not too much. After all, he was a cat. Scaring the chickens away so she could get their eggs without being pecked was quite enough.

As much as she loved her farm, growing up an only child in the middle of rural Florida was living in the middle of nowhere. It was a lonely life. She spent almost two hours each day going to and from grade school. Sighing at the ducks chasing each other, she stretched out flat on her belly on the floor of her tree house. The loudest sound was the faint moo from a distant cow, or the rustling of the leaves around them when a stray breeze blew. "This is the most boring place on Earth. My friends are right. I'm just a dumb bunny on a farm," she complained to Louie for the second time that afternoon. "Those whistling ducks lead more exciting lives than I do." Suddenly far above the lake, a silent, glowing silver streak shot by.

The streak slowed down and turned around, then flew lower, angling back towards them. It circled around the lake, the streak changing into a silver dot as it continued to slow. Finally, flying low over the wild ducks, it headed straight for Adela and Louie.

A small clap of thunder rolled across the clear blue sky, exactly where they'd first seen the streak high above. Adela and Louie jumped, then looked at each other in surprise. The ducks squawked and started flapping to escape, but the silver bullet shot over their heads. The ducks settled back down, whistling in dismay at the unknown intruder.

With a tremendous splash, it landed close to shore, right in front of them. "Louie," Adela whispered slowly, "that's a ... that's a duck." Louie's tail was frozen. He blinked and sniffed at the duck, not knowing what to think. Ducks weren't silver colored. Ducks didn't fly at supersonic speed and make sonic booms. And ducks did not throw up a huge crater of water when they landed. There was something very fishy about this duck ...

It was large for a duck, quite the biggest duck they had ever seen. They watched through the branches as it tried to swim. It struggled to dive, but didn't seem to know how. "What's wrong with this duck?" Adela whispered to Louie. They were both expert duck watchers. They had never seen a duck have the slightest trouble on water.

Finally, the silver duck paddled to shore and disappeared into the low, thick bushes almost directly underneath them. Not wanting to frighten it, Adela and Louie watched very quietly, barely breathing.

They heard rustling sounds from the bushes, then a quiet "quack, quack, quack." Everything was quiet for a few minutes, except for some more rustling noises. Then there was a burst of loud quacking followed by what sounded like "Oh - whew." Adela and Louie looked at each other again with wide eyes.

The silver duck waddled out of the bushes and dove into the water. It seemed to be swimming much better now, and paddled rapidly toward the wild ducks.

As the silver duck drew closer, the wild ducks frantically began to fly away from it. "Oh no!" shouted Adela, jumping up to wave both arms at the silver duck. *Thunk!* Her head slammed into the thick branch over her head, almost knocking her out. "No! Stop! Come back!" A sinister underwater shadow was racing towards the silver duck.

There was an explosion of water and silver feathers. Within seconds, the lake was still and empty. The wild ducks flew away, their frightened whistles and quacks fading slowly into the distance.

3 THE SPACE STATION?

Adela started to cry. "That's the third one," she sobbed, holding the top of her pounding head with both hands. Louie purred, giving her his best wet-nosed kisses and full body rubs. He tried to make her feel better, but she kept crying. A few minutes later, Adela was calm enough to climb down her ladder to the ground. Louie scrabbled backwards down the trunk to a lower branch, then jumped the rest of the way down to stay with her.

A few minutes later a sleek helicopter flew into sight, low and fast over the tree tops. It circled around the lake, then landed on the shore not far from Adela and Louie. The noise from its spinning blades scared Louie, and he ran away. Adela recognized the big blue and white NASA logo painted on the side.

A tall, skinny man wearing large black glasses, his hair thinning and graying around the edges, opened the passenger door and jumped out. He was wearing dark blue overalls with the same light blue NASA logo on the front breast. "Miss," he shouted, running up to her, "Hi, my name is Roger. I'm a scientist from NASA. Have you seen a fast, shiny duck fly this way?"

Adela pointed to the silver feathers still floating on the water and nodded. She tried to talk, but hiccupped instead. The man looked at the feathers through the binoculars hanging from his neck. "What happened?" he asked.

Adela tried to answer, but could only point and sob. Finally, she choked out, "Gator."

The scientist took a laser sensor from his belt and turned it on. He pointed it at the feathers for a minute, inspecting the readout, then ran back to his helicopter. It took off and hovered above the feathers. She saw Roger open his door and lean out, steading himself against the side of the door. He aimed what looked like a very large camera at the feathers.

The helicopter soon returned and landed at the same spot, but Roger remained inside for several minutes after the blades stopped spinning.

When he finally emerged, his head was drooping low as he slowly walked up to Adela. "That was definitely the super-duck," he said in a small voice. "The hyper-spectral image of the feathers confirms it. I'm sorry, miss, I was so excited I didn't even ask your name. Do you live here?"

Adela nodded, rubbing her aching head and wiping away tears. "Adela," was all she could say.

"Hello Adela," Roger said. "Did you see the alligator eat the silver duck?"

Adela nodded again. "That mean alligator keeps trying to eat all my ducks," she sniffled.

The scientist sighed, bent over and took a seat on the thick green grass next to her. They sat together in silence for a moment. Far away one of Adela's cows mooed. Roger stared sadly at the ground.

"Hyper what?" Adela asked in a small voice, trying to change the subject. "Was that the big camera you used?"

"Yes," Roger replied. "That was a hyper-spectral imager," he replied. "It takes special pictures. But instead of taking a picture in just three colors like a regular camera, which uses only red, green, and blue, it takes a picture in about one hundred colors. All at once. That allows you to positively, uniquely identify things, like those feathers." He paused, looking at her. "Almost everything looks different from everything else, if you look at it in a hundred colors."

He gazed down and angled his head, whispering, "I'm so sorry," looking like he was ready to cry himself. "Super-duck was our last hope."

Adela stopped sniffling to look at him. "Super-duck? Why do you call him that?" she asked.

"Her," he said. "For some reason we don't understand, only girl ducks can grow up into super-ducks." Adela stared at him, silently prompting him to continue. "We have been trying to find a way to send cargo and supplies up to the international space station without using big, expensive rockets."

"You see, we have a big problem." He looked at her and sighed again. "This was classified at the highest level, but it doesn't matter now." He squinted into the distance for a minute, fighting back tears, then looked down at her. "You see, over the years, our rockets have become so expensive that we can barely afford to keep flying them. Very few people know this. There are a few companies that try to help us, but in the last few years, many of their rockets have blown up. That made their prices go up. With all the budget cuts to NASA, we are having a hard time keeping the international space station working and supplied." He paused, looking up at the blue sky. "Everything the astronauts consume must be carried up from Earth. We're paying $10,000 to bring them a pound of refried beans. And then we must carry all their waste back to Earth."

He stared at Adela thinking a young girl wouldn't understand, but her eyes bored right back into him, fascinated. "So, we figured out how to genetically engineer a special kind of duck that could fly into space. Each one can carry only a small load, but we could use dozens of them, every day. Or gang them together to carry bigger things. Ducks are environmentally friendly, and the best part is, the only cost is duck feed." He smiled at her. "I know this sounds totally silly."

Adela nodded while she rubbed the top of her head. She had almost stopped sniffling. "Why would she want to fly into space?"

"Most wild ducks migrate south every fall, then fly north, back home, every spring," Roger said. "Secretly, we've been sending super-duck babies back and forth to the space station for years. No one knows but a few people in NASA, the Florida members of Congress, and the President. We believed they would migrate back and forth between Cape Canaveral and the space station. Just like regular ducks migrate. Each one carrying supplies to the space station. We imprinted this trip into their genetic code

---

NASA built and paid for most of the international space station. It orbits around the Earth every 92 minutes, weighs 990,000 pounds, and is the length of a football field (100 yards). Starting in 1998, construction cost approximately 150 billion dollars and took about 13 years to complete.

At any one time, it can house up to 10 astronauts from a variety of countries, living inside a volume roughly equal to a 5 bedroom house. They perform many important scientific experiments that can only be conducted in zero gravity, and others intended to make life better on Earth. But everything they use, eat, drink, and breathe must be carried up from the Earth using large, very expensive rockets. All waste the astronauts generate must be carried back down on same rockets, as there are no dumps in space.

Because it is so close to the Earth, usually around 230 miles high, there is still a tiny bit of atmosphere constantly pulling on it, slowing it down. Therefore, the space station is always slowly falling back towards the Earth. Supply rockets must carry extra fuel and while docked, fire their rockets for seven minutes or more to push the station back up into a higher orbit. The station always keeps a Soyuz emergency escape capsule that can carry a crew of three safely back to Earth.

---

in a way so that their descendants would remember it. Or we thought we did."

"How does she fly so fast?" asked Adela quietly.

"Very good question, young lady," Roger replied. "I don't know. Yet. If we had more time to study her, we could have figured it out. But we had to rush the first test, far ahead of schedule. We weren't ready. And we lost her." He looked like he was fighting back tears again. "Due to an unfortunate set of circumstances, she was the only super-duck we had left."

Roger shifted his skinny bottom to a more comfortable position in the grass. "Right now, we have a serious problem. There are only two toilets on the space station. Last week the second toilet plugged up. The first toilet broke a month ago. Without a proper toilet the astronauts have been using a lot more toilet paper than usual. Now they have run out completely."

Shaking his head slowly, Roger continued. "They have a very stinky situation up there. It's bad. They put all their waste into one room to try to contain the smell, but because of the zero gravity, it keeps floating around. It's a real mess."

He sighed. "Super-duck was bringing plumbing supplies to fix the toilets, and emergency rolls of toilet paper. It would have cost millions of dollars using a big rocket. Which we don't have right now anyway, due to budget cuts."

Roger pulled a handkerchief from his hip pocket. His nose was so large that when he blew it, it sounded like a foghorn. Adela giggled, and he smiled weakly at her.

"Now the President is going to stop the space station program. We can't afford to bring the astronauts the supplies they need to live safely. So, we will have to bring them home in the emergency Soyuz capsule, and abandon the station." Roger folded the handkerchief up and returned it to his pocket. "The space station will fall back towards the Earth soon, and burn up when it re-enters the Earth's atmosphere."

The scientist stared sadly for a few minutes at the small waves lapping on the sandy shore of the lake. Finally, he looked at Adela. "Thank you, young lady," he said. He handed her a small card. "If you ever need me, this has my phone number and email." They stood and he gravely shook her hand. Waving goodbye, he walked slowly back to the helicopter and flew away.

After Roger left, Adela lay in the thick, cool grass gazing at the clear sky, eyes half closed. Birds were chirping fitfully in the mid-day heat, but she did not hear. She was in a space suit tethered to the outside of the space station, busy fixing a critical piece of equipment that had just failed. The pipes from the last working toilet had just plugged shut because the tinkle from her teammates had frozen solid inside. The deathly cold of space had no favorites. She, Adela, was the only one who understood how the complicated space plumbing worked. The fate of the entire crew on board the station was in her hands; even mission control could not help them. By now, her team mates inside the space station were starting to gasp for air because the last working air purifier had overloaded from the smell, she had to hurry …

Meeooow! Adela blinked as Louie's sudden cry brought her back to Earth. Sitting up, she could not see him, but knew he was in the same bushes the silver duck had just visited. She normally understood what Louie's meows meant, but this strange yowl was new. *Meeooow!* Louie never meowed twice unless it was important, so she bounded over to investigate.

Pulling apart the tight branches, she twisted herself through the tangled underbrush. There was Louie, standing next to a crude, unfinished nest scratched into the sandy loam, lined with dead grass and leaves. In it lay a large, silvery egg. Beside the nest lay a highly reflective, large duck-sized backpack, studded with tiny sensors and antennae. Opening the pack, Adela unrolled a pack of small tools and parts, and three little rolls of toilet paper. Each roll was stamped with the blue NASA logo.

They stared at the egg for a long time. "Well," Adela said finally, "We've raised motherless baby bunnies, a starving baby fox, and hundreds of chicks. I've always wanted to raise a duck." She gingerly scooped up the shiny egg, holding it close to her lips. "Why did you land here, little egg, little egg?" she murmured. "Maybe you will grow up and save the astronauts." She looked up at the clear blue sky, searching for the space station. "Those poor astronauts. I'd sure love to be up there. Exploring outer space. Building a house on Mars. Maybe I can help you, little egg." Louie decided he wanted to help raise the duck too, just because he loved Adela so much. He followed her home.

4 THE EGG

Alone with her parents and Louie, Adela lived in the large, rambling two-story farmhouse started by her great-great-grandfather. The inside of the house was mostly wide boards cut from their own trees, now grown dark with the patina of age. Shaded by huge trees and cooled by the breezes from plenty of large windows, Adela never noticed they had no air conditioning. Students from the nearby University of Florida experimented with new types of organic crops, often staying in the cabins scattered throughout the woods. Sometimes they brought thousands of beautiful ladybugs or green lacewings for natural pest control, which was always fun.

Cradling the egg carefully, she ran upstairs to her bedroom. To keep it warm and moist, she quickly made an incubator using a big, thick cardboard box. Switching an old heating pad to low and laying it flat on the bottom, she built a thick nest of clean hay on top, then put a pan of water on the pad next to it. Clamping a light bulb to a metal stand, she placed one of her mother's old thermometers on top of the nest. She adjusted the height of the light bulb and thickness of the straw nest until the thermometer read 99.5 degrees. That was the temperature of their chicken egg incubator, which was close enough for now. Taking the egg from the corner of the box where it was warming, she snuggled it firmly into the center of the nest. Her emergency incubator was complete less than an hour after finding the egg.

Soon after she finished, her mother dropped by for an inspection. "Honey, I really don't think you should try to hatch this," her mother told her, peering over her reading glasses. "You don't want it to happen again." She stared at the egg. "And why did you color it silver?"

"I didn't touch it, honest. Please mom, I really want to do this. I have to." Adela gently touched the egg, now barely warm. "This time I'm going to do it right." She swung her laptop around to show her mother the article she was reading about hatching duck eggs. "See, this is written by the Cornell University duck research laboratory. They have the world's oldest duck disease laboratory, and know everything about raising ducks. I've already created an account." Adela looked up, searching her mother's face for approval.

When Adela was little, she tried to hatch three Rhode Island Red chicken eggs. She didn't know they needed to be turned over several times a day. The chicks never hatched, all dying inside their shell because they were squished flat on one side. It broke Adela's heart, and she cried for days.

Her mother skipped through the Cornell website, thinking it over. "Adela," she said finally, "if it starts to smell, or doesn't hatch in a month, we are throwing it out. Agreed?"

Adela paused, then nodded half-heartedly. Who knew how long a super-duck egg would take to hatch? Roger didn't say. But what choice did she have?

"I'm going into Palatka to pick up some groceries," her mother continued. "Do you want me to see if the feed store has a little humidifier for your incubator, instead of a pan of water?"

Adela nodded again, and started reading everything she could find about hatching baby ducks. She worked on the incubator daily, improving it to ensure the humidity and temperature were kept just right. She carefully turned the egg over four or five times a day, making sure it rested in a different position each time. Louie guarded the box to keep the egg safe from any predators who might sneak in through the window.

A normal duck egg should have hatched in about a month, but Adela knew this wasn't a normal egg. One afternoon when she unexpectedly raced up the stairs and into her room, Adela found her mother hovering over the incubator. As the first month dragged into the second, she began to worry. Adela candled the egg often, a technique thousands of years old but still effective. Waiting until nightfall, she turned out the lights and placed a lit candle behind the egg. By slowly rotating the egg, the candle light shined through the egg, illuminating the tiny embryo inside. It appeared normal, almost like a chicken embryo but larger, with thicker wings and body. Routinely checking it over the following weeks, she was certain it was still growing. It just would not hatch.

Adela's mother normally woke her every day at 5 am to help milk the dairy cows, including school days, unless they had extra help. Her main job was to get the cows ready to hook up to the milking machine, including washing and disinfecting their udders with iodine. Very early one morning, Louie's caterwauling woke her. She jumped up in bed, seeing her mother framed by the hall light. She was carrying the nest with the egg out through her bedroom door. "Mom. No! It's a healthy chick. It's still growing. Please mom," Adela said as she raced to her mother, throwing her arms around her waist. "This is a really special egg. It takes longer."

"Adela, it's been almost 6 weeks, sweetie. I'm afraid it would have hatched by now if it was viable." She bent down and stroked Adela's hair. "I just don't want you to get hurt again. I'm sorry. Honey, it's best this way."

"Mom." Adela began to cry. "Please." Her tears began to drip on her mother's blouse as she sobbed. "Mom. If it goes bad, then you can have it. It's still alive." Adela gave her best shuddering, drawn-out wail, accompanied by plenty of waterworks. "I really want to do this. It's really important. I know it is!"

Her mother sniffed it, then held it up to the hall light. "It's not dark yet, so I suppose we can give it a little longer." She looked at Adela and sighed. "Once you make your mind up, there is no changing it, is there, young lady." Together, they gently placed the nest and egg back in the incubator. "There must be a reason that duck landed here," her mother said softly as she was leaving, "but I sure don't know what it is."

Adela was too upset to fall back asleep, at least for the first minute or two. Then Louie jumped into bed, purring loudly, making a warm spot next to her. "Thanks Louie. What would I do without you." She started to rub him behind the ears, then instantly fell back asleep.

5 THE DUCK

Seven weeks passed. Early one morning, right before her mother's wake-up call, Adela jerked awake when Louie jumped onto her chest. Over his purring, she thought she heard a faint cheep coming from the floor. Turning on the light, she stretched over the edge of the bed and opened the top of the incubator. There was a teensy wet head poking through the shell! It struggled feebly, making the tiniest peeping noises she had ever heard. Louie jumped down to stand next to it, looking like a proud father. From her long experience hatching baby chicks, Adela was able to peel the eggshell off and help the baby duckling emerge without hurting it.

"Look everybody!" A few minutes later Adela ran into the brightly lit kitchen, cradling the baby duckling in the crook of her left arm. "He's not silver at all. He's covered in soft yellow down just like a normal baby duckling. And just look at his beautiful golden eyes."

"Hey, you're kind of cute!" her mother said, stroking the fuzzy duckling's head. "And very late. You should let your father check him over."

Her father was about to head outside to start the day's work. Born with a farmer's instinctive grasp of animal well-being, he had double-majored in animal science and plant science at the University of Florida where he earned honors degrees in both fields. "This is one strange little duck," her father told her, inspecting it closely. He hefted it, holding it up to the light, and shook his head. "Golden eyes? Huh. This is the heaviest chick I've ever seen for its size. Hmm, look at this. The chest is too large. And round." He flipped the downy baby over on its bottom. It remained still, gazing at Adela, not struggling or protesting like a normal chick would. "It's too young to tell if it is a boy or a girl," he continued, "but that's normal. But nothing else is. Let's put this duckling in with the baby chicks. I have a feeling the roosters and hens will protect this little fellow. What is its name?"

For the first time in her life, try as she might, Adela could not think of a name. And she couldn't think of any reason why. Normally the right name popped into her head the moment she saw a new baby animal.

Fortunately, the brood accepted the duckling as one of their own. Over the next few months, Adela spent every spare moment pampering it. Surrounded by baby chicks, the duckling grew up thinking it was a chicken. Sometimes she and Louie played games with the flock. "Where's my bug?" was a favorite. She let the flock see where they hid tasty crickets and worms under a layer of hay or leaves, then led them around the barnyard to confuse them. The goal was to see who then found the treats first. They quickly found it was impossible to fool the duckling; it always remembered where the yummy treats were hidden, gobbling them all.

The long hot summer finally turned to a late fall. Adela's duckling grew into a young duck. As the oak leaves changed color, the fluffy yellow down gave way to an unusual mix of stiff red, brown, black, and white feathers. Its eyes grew a deeper golden color. Adela's father would shake his head whenever he saw it, calling it a mutt, or a genetic mutation.

Adela was born having a deep empathy with her animals. Holding them, peering deep into their eyes, she unconsciously emptied her mind, reaching out for their thoughts. Occasionally, for just a minute, she could almost become the animal, feeling its feelings, thinking its thoughts. These were always simple, innocent thoughts, with none of the distractions she normally carried in her head. No homework due tomorrow, no sick calf to worry about. It was a welcome relief from her human life. When she was very little she had occasionally alarmed her parents by behaving like that animal, forgetting who she was.

Some evenings, her other animals fed and put to bed, Adela would concoct silly evening serenades for her duck. Sitting in her lap, gazing into each other's eyes, she would sing to it softly. "Little duck, little duck, why did you land here? There were so many places both far and near. What will you do, what will you see? Why were you sent here to be with me?" Her little duck, still nameless, was perfectly happy to sit in the warmth and love of her lap.

Like most animals, the duck's independence increased as it grew older. As the mild winter set in it stopped following Adela around the farm, no longer always trying to keep her in sight. One day it gathered the courage to swim out to the flock of wild ducks. Nearly skewering the hapless duck, the wild ducks firmly rebuffed it, with the loss of several colorful feathers as a painful reminder. It was very patient, however, trying again day after day.

It learned to paddle just out of pecking range, waiting, watching, learning about life as a wild duck. After several weeks, the flock grudgingly began to accept it, first as an intruding outsider, and eventually as part of their family. It started swimming all day with the wild ducks. One day, the flock finally allowed it to fly away with them. Adela never learned where they went. Wherever it was, they always returned dutifully at dusk, whistling and quacking as they came in for their evening splashdown.

6 THAT ALLIGATOR, ONCE AGAIN

One afternoon, the week before Christmas vacation started, Adela was walking to history class with her best friend Jessica. "Adela, I have to see this duck. I love your crazy story about finding the silver egg. It really lets you carry it around? What is its name?"

Adela frowned, grabbing at the thick history book sliding out of her arms. "We still can't tell if he's a boy or girl. My dad says there's never been a duck like this. So, I can't name him yet." When Jessica didn't answer, Adela continued. "I call him a him because he acts like a boy duck. He's not an "it", he's way too smart."

"Well, I've never been on a real farm before," Jessica paused. "Can I come over Saturday and see the animals? Maybe sleep over?"

Jessica would be her first visitor in almost three years. Adela's father suggested that Jessica help with the chores to understand how a working farm operated. However, Adela could take the day off if she wanted.

Jessica's mother dropped her off early Saturday morning. Adela gave her the full tour. They hunted stray eggs laid by naughty hens who refused to lay in the coop. These straying hens had a tendency to end up as meals for the local possums, raccoons, and foxes, so the girls drove as many as they could into a coop. Jessica kept a dozen eggs to show her parents how much better they tasted than store eggs. Leaving the chicken coops, Adela guided Jessica to a barn having a tall silo nestled against one side.

"Jess, here's where we make the silage for the cows. Hay, oats, alfalfa, whole plants, everything goes in the top of this big silo and ferments so it's yummy for the cows. When it's ready, we pull it out using this ramp here at the bottom."

Jessica paused, not following Adela as she started up the ladder on the side of the silo. "Didn't you say there were dangerous gases inside? I can smell it from here. Can we go see the cows instead?"

They skipped into the woods, a shortcut to the heifer pasture. Wandering through the big trees, Adela stopped to climb her childhood favorite, followed by Jessica. It was a tremendous, ancient live oak that afforded a great view of the gently rolling countryside. Some of the lower branches were thicker than the trunks of most trees. The birds seemed to grow joyous around the girls as they climbed and played in the tree, their songs trumpeting the happiness of young life. Adela wrapped Spanish moss around her face. "Jessica, who am I?" Jessica laughed, shaking her head. "Graybeard, the chicken pirate! Grrrhh!"

Jumping down from Adela's tree, they walked through an aisle formed by two rows of massive trees. "You said these next cows are heifers, right? What are they, babies?" questioned Jessica, holding her hair back as she ducked a low branch. "Are they dangerous?"

"No, not really, unless the mother is there to protect her," Adela replied as they approached the clearing. "The mom can come after you. But this herd is only heifers, no moms." Without slowing, Adela flipped herself over a fencepost in a single smooth motion. Calling back over her shoulder from the pasture, she continued. "Heifers are young female cows who have never had a baby. Leia! Bessie! Sugar!" Over a dozen juvenile cows started trotting up. "You know I've got treats, don't you? One sugar cube each. Yes, I'm sorry, that's all for today." After Jessica struggled over the wire mesh fence, Adela passed her a handful of sugar cubes. The young cows were tranquil, eating the candy from the girl's hands. Jessica squealed with delight as the soft, smooth wet noses nuzzled her hands, with the occasional gentle moo from a well-placed rub behind the ears.

The meadow curved through the woods to a wooden gate, leading to a much larger pasture for the main herd of dairy cows. Well-marked, neatly fenced-in fields of lettuces, bell pepper, eggplant, and broccoli lay on both sides of the pasture. "These vegetables are all organic, right?" asked Jessica. "What do you use for fertilizer?"

"Everything's organic. The University has used these fields for years. They rent half our farm for growing new kinds of crops that don't use pesticides. My great-great-grandfather didn't believe in using pesticides. Or his son or anyone else since then, so our soil is what the University calls 'pristine.' They say they have a hard time finding soil that has never had any pesticides or artificial fertilizer. They love our fertilizer. It's made of really good organic compost. We compost our cow manure in an old silo with the plants we don't use for feed, and broadcast it out with a spreader," replied Adela. "We grow almost everything the cows eat right here."

"Eeeww," responded Jessica, holding her nose as they passed downwind of a freshly fertilized field. A little further, the green meadow opened into a clearing next to the lake. "I don't see any ducks," Jessica said, scanning the lake as they approached. "Do you know when they will be back?"

"They normally come back when it starts getting dark," replied Adela, surveying the water as she stopped by the edge. Jessica stood back several feet from shore, remembering Adela's story about the alligator. Taking her farm boots and thick socks off, Adela walked out almost to her knees and sighed, wiggling her toes in the sandy bottom. "Come on in, the water feels great. Nice and cool."

"Adela, didn't you say there was an alligator in this pond?"

"Yeah, but I can't figure out where he lives," she answered. Then she froze. Perhaps seventy-five feet away, rising so slowly she hadn't noticed, a pair of dark eyes surfaced. Hidden in a patch of lily pads, they might be watching her. They did not blink. As Adela stared into them, she automatically tried to sense what the alligator was feeling. But the shadowy eyes seemed dead, lifeless; nobody home.

She knew the alligator had no chance of catching her, even if he charged. She was too big, he was too far away, and the water near her was too shallow for him to hide. As she continued to gaze at him, concentrating, she finally felt a slight sensation. It was like she was standing in the waterfalls of a river, eyes closed, senses cut off from the outside world by the water pounding down around her. The perception seemed to crystallize into a faint unthinking, all-consuming purpose, but she could not figure out what it was.

She focused all her attention on those joyless eyes, and what was behind them. Squinting, her eyes almost closed, she slowly felt a faint, gray image forming in her mind. The fuzzy feeling reminded her of Thanksgiving, where she was waiting at the dinner table to get the big crispy turkey drumstick she loved. With a start, she suddenly realized it was her own legs that were so appetizing. The emotion she was feeling was nothing more than single-minded, all-consuming hunger. She laughed softly, imagining how she could bend over to eat her own drumsticks. And they weren't even crispy.

"Jess, there he is," she whispered. Knowing the alligator was timid, like all wild animals, Adela raised her arm slowly to point so he would not run away and hide.

Jessica searched the water carefully. "Are those two dark spots his eyes?" she finally asked. "The alligator?" When Adela nodded, Jessica shrieked and ran towards the house. Leaving a small ripple, the alligator immediately bolted underwater. Adela watched closely for a minute, until she was certain the small waves and rustling lily pads were heading away from her. *Yes, you are a big scaredy-cat, just like I thought,* she said to herself. *Just a big coward who eats helpless little ducks.* Louie, who had followed the girls at a distance all afternoon, calmly continued his bath as Jessica ran by.

7 JESSICA AND THE BULL

"Jess, can you fill these feeders with crushed oyster shell? Here's the bag. The chickens eat it to make their eggshells thick and strong." Adela found the best way to convince Jessica she was never in danger from the alligator was to keep her busy with farm chores. "I don't know why, but my duck eats more oyster shell than the chickens."

After the girls gathered the chicken eggs from the largest coop, Adela showed Jessica how to run some of them through a machine that gently brushed the hay off each one, without washing them. "Adela, don't you wash these eggs before you sell them?"

"We wash most of them, because they go to regular stores. But these we don't. If you wash them, they get old quickly. And they don't taste as good. Then you have to keep them in the refrigerator like regular eggs. Almost everyone else washes them, just so they look better." She looked up to see if Jessica was comprehending. "You see, when each egg is laid, it comes out of the chicken coated with something that protects it from the air. My dad says it's an oxygen barrier or something, and it keeps them fresh. If you wash the egg, you wash off that coating. I've cooked unwashed eggs that sat out warm for three weeks, and eggs fresh from the chicken. You can't tell the difference."

As they left the coop, Jessica looked around and tossed back her long blond hair. "Why don't you have horses? All my friends do, and they don't have nearly this much land."

"We have a bull I rode when he was little," Adela said hopefully. "Sampson. Three years ago, I entered him in the county fair. The two-year old class. He won second prize. And he's sweet. Let's go say hi to him."

Sampson's pasture was on the other side of Adela's house, barely visible from the chicken coops. Climbing through the wooden railings of Sampson's split rail fence, Jessica got her first close look at him. Brown and white, Sampson was tallest just ahead of his front legs, with a massive chest that was much thicker than his hindquarters. He looked almost like a big cartoon character, with huge muscles up front.

"He's beautiful. And really big." Jessica slowed her pace, watching the bull as it stared back at her. Sampson started turning sideways to track Jessica as she walked. "Adela, he's looking at me like he doesn't like me."

Adela continued further into Sampson's pasture, both pleased and distracted by Jessica's interest. Prattling happily, she was not giving Sampson the close attention she normally did. "Oh, he always does that," she said over her shoulder, remembering the games they used to play. "Just scratch him under the chin, and he's your friend for life. Better yet, give him one of these sugar cubes. Hey, Sampson!" The bull was still focused on Jessica, circling to face her as she advanced.

Jessica finally stopped, uncertain what to do. Adela proceeded blithely on, walking up to the bull. Louie stayed under the fence, wondering why Adela was doing this. For the few last years, she had instructions from her father not to enter his pasture without having a truck or tractor nearby for cover. Just in case. As bulls grew older, they could become unpredictable. Adela knew this.

Louie thought Adela took far too many chances. When still a kitten, Adela's father had told Louie very firmly, many times, that his only job was to look after Adela. Adela's father had a natural way with the animals on the farm. They instinctively understood what he needed. The care and respect he gave them generated an unshakable trust. But he couldn't always be there to keep an eye on Adela. The farm was a big place, and he made Louie understand that he was the only one that was always around to keep Adela safe. The farm employed various workers around the year, but they rarely had the time to watch her.

The bull pawed once at the ground, snorted, then lowered his head and slowly started to gallop toward Jessica. Adela, sugar cubes in hand, stopped and turned, mouth open, as Sampson passed her. Adela had seen him charge only once in his life – last fall, a poor rabbit dared to eat his sweetest grass, only to be scared out of a years' growth. Jessica stared, frozen in place, as the immense horns pounded towards her. For her time stopped, but the bull did not. He seemed to gain speed every instant, but she could not move an inch.

A second later Louie cannon-balled into Jessica's thigh, a projectile of rock-solid muscle knocking her sideways, then streaked towards Sampson at light speed. Louie was snarling like a miniature lion as he flew onto the field. The impact and howling startled Jessica out of her trance, saving her life. Adrenaline suddenly coursing through her veins, she pivoted and sprinted for the fence.

Hissing and spitting, Louie leaped in front of Sampson. The bull never even saw him. Sampson was entirely focused on driving the unknown intruder from his territory. At the last split-second Louie dived out of the way with the agility only a cat possesses, the mammoth hooves almost trampling him into pussycat paste. Jessica leap madly and dove under the bottom rail of the fence only a few yards ahead of the enraged animal. Sampson thundered on, angling away at the last second, almost smashing the fence to matchsticks. The tip of one horn grazed the middle railing, scoring a deep gouge while knocking it free from its posts. The heavy wooden beam *thunked* as one end slammed into the ground inches from Jessica's head.

It was all over in seconds. Adela gawked in disbelief as Sampson, barely slowing, rounded his turn and headed toward her. It slowly dawned on her that this was not the friendly, albeit somewhat dumb friend she grew up with. This was a different animal, one she did not know after all, very angry and heading straight for her. The sudden joy of re-living their old games vanished as she finally decided to bolt for the fence, Sampson angling in right behind.

By now Sampson was snorting, blind with rage and charging anything in his space. With a quick hand on top of the nearest post, Adela gracefully hurdled over the fence with two full seconds to spare, although she stumbled and fell upon landing. She watched dumbfounded as Sampson trotted back to his original spot, shaking his head. Upon arriving at his home station near the middle of the field, Sampson turned and watched them. His range was now safe; all was right with the world. Calmly turning around, he swished his tail and ears as if nothing ever happened. Adela jumped up. Dusting her hands off, she headed towards Jessica. "Well, this is the most excitement I've had all month!"

On her first attempt to stand Jessica made it only halfway, legs buckling to deposit her back on the ground. Grabbing the fence, she pulled herself up and shakily stood erect. Adela drew closer, so she would not have to shout. "Sorry about that. He's never acted this way before." She didn't notice Jessica's face, tanned by the Florida sun like her own, was white, her entire body trembling. "It must be because he's never seen you before."

Jessica took several deep breaths, trying to calm herself. "Adela, he almost killed me." She finally looked Adela in the eye, tears in her own. "Didn't you realize this could happen? Are you really that stupid?"

"I can't believe he did that." Adela's face twisted when she heard the emotion in Jessica's voice. Sampson was one of her favorite childhood playmates. When they were both about the same size, Sampson being only a few months old, one of their favorite games was to charge and head-butt each other. He wouldn't hurt a fly. "He's really a sweetie. Next time we'll make sure he knows who you are before we go into his pasture." Adela paused, unsure what to do or say. "It's OK. I'm sorry, Jess. Mom probably has lunch ready." Adela started walking home.

Jessica stared at Adela's retreating back, again frozen in place with disbelief. "Come on, let's go see what there is to eat," Adela called again over her shoulder. Jessica stood transfixed, then, shaking her head, slowly followed.

Louie sat well away from the fence, narrowly watching Adela walk away. All he could think of was to give himself a nervous bath of half-hearted licks. Adela's risk-taking behavior had to stop. But how?

Once inside, Adela raided the refrigerator while Jessica went straight to the bathroom. Pouring them each a glass of cold whole milk, the cream floating on top, Adela paused outside the partly open bathroom door. She wanted to ask Jessica what she felt like for lunch, but Jessica was talking on her phone.

"Mom? Will you come pick me up?" Adela heard Jessica sniffling, then, "Yes right now. NOW. No, it's not. Are you coming? OK, bye."

Adela slumped back against the wall, too stunned to talk. Animals had chased her all her life; it was part of growing up on a farm. As long as you understood them, you were fine. Surely, being chased by an ornery bull, who was really a sweetheart inside, was not such a big deal. Was it?

8 SUPER DUCK!

Christmas vacation was the busiest time of year for many local farmers. In the normally warm Florida climate, the cool weather was the best time to plant peas, beets and broccoli, and prune the baby blueberry bushes planted the prior winter. Adela was so busy helping to seed and fertilize, she eventually forgot all about Jessica's visit. Until the first day of school. Jessica appeared wearing blingy new overalls, shiny cowboy boots, and a fashionable straw hat.

At first glance, Jessica's stiff blue overalls made her think of her own soft, comfortable overalls at home. Wearing them was like wrapping herself in her favorite warm childhood blanket, making her happy on the inside. But Jessica had surrounded herself with friends, and was pointedly ignoring Adela. "I guess spending your whole life around dumb farm animals rubs off," Jessica said as Adela hovered nearby. "Stupid is as stupid does." Hiding her numbed emotions, Adela kept to herself and cried quietly all day. Starting that day, school stopped being her private refuge from the loneliness of the farm.

Adela never had many close friends, but by mid-January she was certain most classmates were avoiding her. What really hurt was the cold shoulder from her former best friend. Two years earlier, for "what I want to be when I grow up" day in fourth grade, Adela had worn her favorite farm clothes to school. She never imagined her classmates would secretly make fun of her as the country bumpkin for weeks afterwards. She tried to forgive them, but never was able to completely forget.

Secretly, Adela always yearned to be like Jessica; glamorous, well-dressed, and popular. She knew she would never join the country club Jessica's parents belonged to, with its swimming pool and golf course. Because Jessica joined the track team, Adela also joined in fourth grade. But this backfired. Adela was easily the strongest and fastest girl on the team, even outrunning the boys. But she quickly learned that always winning created more resentment than admiration. The trick was to let other girls win, without making it obvious.

One night in February, about a month after Christmas vacation ended, her duck did not return. By the third night after his disappearance, Adela's stomach was hurting so badly her parents excused her from school the next day. This was the first day of school she ever missed in her life. In another first, her father excused her from chores, so she could sleep in. At dawn on the fourth morning, Adela jerked awake. The shock came from a cold wet nose freezing the inside of her ear, but the warm, breathy purring told her everything was really all right.

Rubbing her eyes open, Louie was already waiting for her, dimly outlined in her bedroom doorway. His tail was straight out, the end swishing quickly in his cocky "come on, let's go!" swing. *Meeooow!* "You crazy cat, don't bother me. I'm sick," she mumbled. She started to lay back down, then the memory struck her. "Oh, wait – I know that yowl." Barefoot and dressed in pajamas, she threw the covers off and started running full tilt after him.

Louie raced downstairs through the kitchen, then flew through his cat door to wait impatiently on the back porch until Adela appeared. Zipping down the path to the lake as soon as she cleared the back door, he stopped a few feet from shore. There was her duck, floating only about thirty feet out. Adela skidded to a stop next to him in shock, hand flying to her mouth. "Louie! He's molted, and turned silver! The poor thing must be starving. Let's bring him inside." Without thinking she rapidly waded into the water, soaking the legs of her pajamas. "We'll have father look at him and see if he's hurt."

Louie watched closely, ears back, tail frozen downward. Adela's father had told her since she was little not to wade into the lake if an alligator was living there.

Unexpectedly the dead eyes suddenly flashed through her mind, stopping her mid-step in the thigh-deep water. She felt she shared a deep bond with Sampson, and had always assumed he would never hurt her. Shock coursed through her as she realized that afternoon with Jessica, Sampson shared the same mindless eyes as the alligator. Unthinking, with the same deadly purpose lurking behind them.

But her duck was floating only a few yards ahead, looking at her calmly. Waiting for her to come pick him up. Adela looked around in every direction, trying to peer into the water. The sun was still kissing the horizon, keeping the water impenetrably black. She could not see a thing beneath the surface. But, this would only take a second. She strode forward rapidly, the water swirling around her as she went deeper.

Using his better-than-human eyes, the orange light of dawn revealed a long shadow racing from the lily pads toward Adela. By now she was up to her waist, reaching for the duck. Louie jumped straight up, yowling his loudest immediate-danger alarm. Adela stopped abruptly, outstretched hands almost reaching the duck, and looked around. Inhaling cat-quick while still in mid-air, Louie howled again at the top of his lungs, triggering both Adela and the duck to finally react.

With every ounce of her strength, Adela vaulted up and backwards toward shore. The silver duck threw himself straight up into the air in a frenzy of flapping. An instant later, the water between them exploded. A huge snout studded with 80 razor-sharp teeth slammed shut with bone-splintering force, exactly where the duck rested a second earlier. It seemed to miss each of them by inches. The duck quickly gained a few feet of altitude and flew to the farthest side of the lake, too frightened even to quack.

Once on shore Adela stood catching her breath, peering out over the water. The gator was nowhere in sight, not even a ripple. "Thanks Louie," she panted, bending down to rub him behind the ears with dripping wet hands. He shook his head in annoyance from the water and backed away from her. She straightened and stepped back, squinting for the alligator. "What a coward. Well, he's gone. Let's get the four-wheeler and go around the lake. I'll bring the bag of duck feed and call him," she said as they headed to the barn. "That'll bring him in."

Louie was still badly frightened. He would have jumped into the water to protect her, but after all, it *was* water. He was a cat. Besides, the alligator would have ignored him; that alligator liked ducks. Most important of all, Adela would be left alone, with no one to protect her.

"Dad, that alligator is back," Adela told her father later that morning, handing him the silver bird. "He almost ate this silly duck. Can you see if he's OK?"

Her father took one look and whistled. Being a 6th generation farmer, his instinctive feel for the health of animals was well known. The few veterinarians who visited marveled at his ability to diagnose the problems they missed. Clearing a side table of books, he gently stretched the duck out under a lamp. Adela preened the stiff, unbending silver feathers on his neck and head, while crooning soothing duck talk to calm her baby.

"Well, young lady," he said several minutes later, "Your he is actually a she. She is fine. These silver-colored feathers are light as a feather, but hard as a rock. They are like a protective shield around her," he continued, lifting a wing and probing gently with his stethoscope. "Her skin is thick - this is not normal duck skin, it's made of layers of something really slippery and extremely tough. And her chest seems to be hollow, but lined with something hard." He cocked his head sideways, feeling deeply with his fingers. "Like a tin can." He shook his head and laughed. "This is impossible." The bird finally reacted by squawking in protest. He looked up at Adela, removing his stethoscope. "I wish I had an X-ray machine.

I've never seen anything like this in my life."

Adela's eyes shined, the name of her golden-eyed duck finally coming in a flash. She was the Phoenix.

Mid to late winter was the best time of the year for planting and harvesting many vegetables, especially the leafy greens. The following Saturday, Adela was pouring a bag of spinach seed into the seed drill on their smaller John Deere tractor. High over the lake, out of the corner of her eye, she thought she saw a silver streak. She dropped the bag, spilling the tiny seeds all over the ground and hoped, holding her breath. After what seemed an eternity, a long, fading thunderclap sounded across the open blue sky. Adela finally exhaled noisily, a long, happy sigh, tears leaking down her cheeks.

On Monday she was cheerful and content, surprising classmates accustomed to a morose, withdrawn Adela. After saying hi to Jessica three times that day only to be ignored, Adela stopped her in the hallway as their last class of the day filed out. "Hey Jess, I'm really sorry about what happened with Sampson. I should have realized he didn't know you. We should never have gone into his pasture. You're right, I was stupid, and I wanted to say I'm sorry." Jessica didn't know how to reply, so she mumbled something about it being OK. After that, Jessica and her friends decided it was no longer entertaining to make fun of Adela. And Adela began to realize she no longer needed school as much as she had before. She already had what really mattered.

Like most local Florida farmers in mid-winter, Adela's parents were simply too busy to listen to the news, other than the weather. Adela found TV news boring, preferring to occasionally listen to overseas stations on their shortwave radio in the pre-dawn darkness. No one heard the strange local news reports cropping up over the next several weeks.

"Last night, here in north central Florida, a local astronomer reported seeing a glowing silver streak shooting up into space," the TV newsman reported. "Yes, folks, I said up, not down. Not a meteor. It was less than a hundred miles north of Cape Canaveral, but no rocket was launched last night – I called a friend there and checked to see if there were any classified night missions. The astronomer said he has no explanation for what it could be. Possibly a UFO?"

A few weeks later, the 11 o'clock news from Gainesville ran the following story. "Last night, an astronaut on the international space station reported being awakened by a tapping on the window above her sleeping bag. She said she sat up and saw what appeared to be a large duck, colored silver, floating outside her window in space." The announcer smiled at his companion like he didn't believe it either, twisting his head while rolling and widening his eyes like he was going cuckoo. "Apparently, it was pecking at the thick glass. When she woke another astronaut to witness this rather strange event, the bird was gone. Having been on the station now for almost a year, the astronaut clearly is suffering from a case of acute space sickness. NASA has decided to return her to Earth but unfortunately, after the failures of both of the last two supply missions, all flights to the space station are grounded. She is currently being held on board the space station under close observation." The announcer turned and looked at his blond co-host with raised eyebrows. "Where else would she go?"

9 ROGER RETURNS

For weeks, Adela had noticed that Phoenix would hum loudly right before rocketing off at supersonic speed. One Friday afternoon after school, she decided it was time to text Roger at NASA with the details. He called her right back. "Oh my gosh. Really? Are you sure?" Roger asked. "Can you catch her and have her ready for me? Do you have a place where we can test her?" He sounded very excited, but highly stressed. "This is actually perfect timing, with the latest problem on the space station. We will have to work as hard as we can. We are almost out of time." Roger paused, and Adela heard him mutter something that sounded like, "we have to try." Then Roger took a deep breath and blew it out slowly, sounding more cheerful. "Phoenix, what a great name. I'll be there right after dawn tomorrow morning. Thanks Adela!"

"Oh no, Adela please, not another potato battery," her father groaned Friday night when she started to ask him about this year's upcoming science fair project. "I am not doing this again." Adela still had no idea what to do, and her project was due in two weeks. She was beginning to worry. The science fair project had become an annual battle with her parents.

"Dad, Dr. Roger White from NASA wants to come over and measure my duck," interrupted Adela. "I always told you she was a very special duck. I'm going to help him figure out why she flies so fast." Adela's father had seen the duck fly at supersonic speed and agreed, with relief, that this testing would be perfect for her project. He gave her the weekend off, and she spent Friday evening cleaning up their messy, barn-sized workshop. She made a pen in the very back corner for Phoenix, and stored her safely with plenty of food, water, and hay.

The next morning, Adela finished her milking chores shortly before dawn. While eating breakfast, she kept a sharp lookout from the kitchen window down their mile-long driveway. She and her father often listened to international news programs together on the shortwave radio in the kitchen while it was still dark, but he was already outside planting carrots.

Over the years they rigged up an elaborate high-gain antenna system, picking up stations from all over the world. Suddenly she froze in shock, breakfast burrito half-way to her mouth. "… astronauts only discovered yesterday that the fuel from the emergency Soyuz escape capsule had leaked out, rendering it useless," said the clipped Kiwi voice of Radio New Zealand International, oscillating with the distance. "Six days from now, the space station should begin to contact the outermost layers of the Earth's atmosphere. By then, it will have become too hot and turbulent for a rescue attempt, as any rocket docking with the station would be swept away. One to two days after this, the forces from the atmosphere acting across the unequally shaped structure will tear it apart. The larger pieces will re-enter the atmosphere individually. Most are expected to be completely incinerated before impact, but some larger pieces could survive to strike the Earth." The announcer paused. "There is no comment from the three astronauts on board." A wave of fear washed over Adela. So this was the latest problem Roger mentioned.

As dawn broke, the faint plume of dust she was looking for began rising in the distance. She ran outside while finishing her favorite warm egg, melted cheese, green chili and potato breakfast burrito, one of her mother's specialties.

Roger rolled up in a large, very strange looking car stuffed full of scientific equipment. A massive, shiny copper cylinder, covered with intricate wiring and strange gadgets, was strapped on the roof. She waved him into the big workshop next to the barn, staring at his car with wide eyes as he passed. "Those windows don't roll down, do they?" she asked, suspecting he could not hear through the thick glass that looked suspiciously like portholes. What a car!

After parking in the workshop, she walked around the car. In spite of the depressing news about the space station she could not help laughing; this was truly the original nerd mobile. It looked like a giant black Oscar Meyer wiener from space, only laying straight, not curved up like a hot dog. Instead of a normal windshield, it had a row of thick trapezoidal-shaped windows embedded across the front sloping panel of the car. The round sides curved up to join at the short flat roof, which was only about three feet wide. The same trapezoidal glass windows were studded down the lengths of both sides, and across the curving rear. Although black, the body had an over-coat of clear shellac that shined through the fresh dust from her driveway.

She rapped the side of the car with her knuckles. It was hard, but did not sound like metal. She already knew Roger was a crazy scientist, but this was too much. "Roger, do you want to turn this car into a spaceship?"

Roger laughed with her. "I've been working on turning this car into a submarine car for fifteen years now. I can't afford the two million dollars a normal one costs. I've already built three single-seater experimental aircraft from carbon fiber materials." He looked down at her and smiled. "You didn't know I was a licensed pilot, did you?" Adela shook her head, grinning. What a mad scientist. He could be in a movie.

"Ever since I saw the James Bond movie where he drives his submarine car out of the water and hands the spectator a fish, I wanted to make my own submarine car." He looked up at the ceiling. "It was 'The Spy Who Loved Me,' I believe. James drove a Lotus. He had Q around to make his submarine car, but we have a world-class machine shop at Kennedy Space Center I use on nights and weekends. And we're right next to the ocean for testing."

Roger knocked on the roof with his knuckles. "I started with this nice, big, powerful 1969 Plymouth Fury I had when I was a teenager. I made the outer body from carbon-fiber shells of old rocket payload shrouds, lightweight and strong. Space qualified." Rapping the windows, he continued, "Fused silica, quadruple-layer windows that are early rejects from the space station – but still immensely strong. Plenty safe, even micrometeorite proof. And everything was free, all this was going to be thrown away."

He opened a rear door cut into the round shell of its side, leaned in, and handed Adela a crate filled with electronics from the jumble within. "See where I took the back seats out? That's almost a thousand pounds of 48-Volt lithium batteries bolted down right there. There is more stretched out under the whole length of this temporary floor. They are enough to drive the wheels when on land, and in the water power the jets, heaters, everything."

Roger passed Adela another crate, then crawled under the car to point at two long indentations in the bottom. "The water jets used to be right here, to lift the car up when it was underwater. This car is as heavy as a rock, and it would stay on the bottom if I didn't have something to lift it. I'd get stuck. So I used two electric pumps that were part of an old rocket motor, pumping water instead of liquid rocket fuel. They provide enough thrust to effectively make the car weightless when underwater." He smiled sheepishly as Adela cocked her head sideways. "Oh, they worked, the two times I tried it in the ocean. Only not as well as I'd hoped."

When Adela opened her eyes wide at him, he grinned at her and continued. "I went in the ocean at Cape Canaveral, but didn't go very far, or very deep. Just offshore. I took the jets off last night to lighten the car, along with the brass propellers mounted on the outside." He pointed behind the batteries, past where the rear seat should have been. "And there are the three big compressed air tanks. This should be more than enough air for two people to stay underwater for three hours."

Roger stood up and stretched his long body, arms over his head. "I designed it to be streamlined for water, so this car should be somewhat aerodynamic for flying through air. I've tested it underwater and could not find a drop of water inside, so I know it's watertight. I hope it is also airtight." When she didn't look convinced, he laughed again. "I know it sounds totally crazy. But that's what I do in my spare time. I don't have any family to go home to at night. It keeps me sane." When Adela's head snapped around to stare at him with wide eyes, he added quietly, "I think." She smiled.

After Adela cleared more workbench space, they started unpacking his car in earnest. "I've been busy researching why Phoenix flies so fast," Roger said, carefully unstrapping the copper cylinder from the roof. "I have brought her old test equipment, and a few new items as well. If we can figure out how the super-duck drive works, I brought the basics to try to build our own space drive." Adela didn't say anything.

They unloaded for a few more minutes in the peace and quiet found only on a farm, invisible cows lowing and mooing softly through the early morning ground fog. Phoenix, nosing around in her hay, quacked quietly once in a while. Snoozing over their heads on a wide, dusty wood beam, Louie chased mice in his dreams. "If we do figure it out, would you happen to have the parts and tools we need to build a super-duck space drive here? In my car?" Adela's silence continued, her face scrunched into doubt.

Roger tried again. "Remember when the toilets on the space station broke?" When she nodded, he continued, "We managed to get them two supply ships during the past eight months. We thought that fixed the toilets permanently, but three months ago, no, almost four months ago, they failed in a completely different way. They have no parts to fix it."

Roger pulled an old chair next to her and sat down, searching her face. "The astronauts have been piling up their waste, then blowing it out into space. Which they are not supposed to do, for several reasons. One is that they lose a tiny bit of air every time they do this, and now they don't have any extra air left. So, for the last few months they have been storing the waste in a sealed room, and it's been building up." Roger sighed. "I know this doesn't sound important. Or very nice. But it has been decomposing, creating methane gas. The methane has grown to a potentially explosive level in that room. And there is electrical circuitry in almost every wall. If they get a spark, it could blow up the space station, and kill them all."

Adela had been very quiet, thinking, but could wait no longer. "Roger, are you going to hurt Phoenix?"

Roger's head jerked up at the directness of her question. Slowly lowering it, he replied, "I'm not going to lie to you. The fact is, about one-third of the super-ducks we tested in the past died." When Adela started violently shaking her head no, he interrupted. "We must pass electrical current through certain parts of her control and flight mechanisms to measure their response. There is no other way to figure out how this works. In the past, sometimes it stopped their hearts. But now we have learned how to use less current, and still get ..."

Adela interrupted him, striding over to the pen she made for Phoenix. "No. You never said anything about killing her." She opened the pen and stood aside. Phoenix stood looking at them uncertainly, then started waddling awkwardly through the big shop towards the door.

Roger followed, placing his hand on her shoulder. "Adela. You didn't let me finish. We have recalculated the amount of electricity needed. We can now chirp the frequency and use far less current. She should be fine. I promise." Adela remained silent, her expressive face showing extreme doubt.

Rogers lips pressed together tightly, his face showing the extreme strain he was feeling. "There is a second problem. The space station drops about 300 feet every day. This is from the normal drag due to the tiny bit of atmosphere up there. The station has no rockets of its own to boost itself back up. Supply rockets provide the only means of raising its orbit. After they dock with the station, they usually fire for several minutes to boost it. Because there have been almost no supply rockets, it has steadily dropped and will soon re-enter the atmosphere and burn up. It is already at a dangerously low altitude."

Roger stood and paced around the workshop. "I've brought the parts with me the astronauts need for the toilet. We have had them ready for months. Inventing a space-car to deliver them is, well, a dream, I know. It's completely nuts." He sat again, looking at her with a sad smile. "But with the last two rockets blowing up, we're grounded. If the toilet cannot be fixed within the next three days, they are ordered to abandon the station, using the emergency Soyuz capsule."

Adela leaned her head back to look up at Roger, meeting his eye. "I just heard the Soyuz had no fuel. They can't use it. And the space station is about to enter the atmosphere. Those astronauts are going to die."

Roger returned Adela's look with one of surprise, horror flashing across his face. "How did you hear that? It was not supposed to be announced until tomorrow morning." When she did not answer but continued to look at him, Roger shook his head in defeat. "Well, I'm glad you know. That is why I dropped everything and came over here today. If the space station is destroyed, the astronauts will die terrible deaths. It's worse than that, even." Roger sighed sadly. "A death blow to the entire manned space program. We may never get back into space."

Adela leaned against the car, watching Phoenix as she slowly duck-walked out of the shop, quacking quietly the same way a chicken clucks to itself. "Just how sure are you Phoenix will be safe?"

"Adela, there is very little chance it will stop her heart. She is much stronger than our super-ducks were, because here she has lived an outdoor life. Our ducks lived in the lab, and took very little exercise. Exercise has a huge impact on the health of the heart. Phoenix is so strong and healthy, I'm almost positive it won't hurt her at all." Roger stood, then stared at his feet. "But to be totally honest, there is always that chance." He looked up at her. "The decision is yours."

Then it struck her. *My mom always says things happen for a reason*, she thought. *Why did the silver duck pick this place?* She shook her head as everything crystallized inside her, suddenly making sense. *This is why Phoenix came here.* She had never been so certain of anything in her life. *I have to do this. I'm meant to do this.* A gut feeling washed over her, as immutable as sunrise. *Phoenix will be fine. I know it.* She turned to catch Phoenix before she reached the lake.

"I help my dad rebuild the tractors and combines every year," she replied, stopping at the door. "Not just the engines, but the threshers, PTO's, everything." She mentally reviewed their stock of tools and parts. "And we had to fix the milking station last winter by ourselves because the repairman was out sick all winter with mono. We have a drill press, router, lathe, bandsaw, TIG welder, ..." She stopped speaking as she realized for the first time, she was no longer ashamed of being raised on a farm.

"This is a farm," she finished. "A really good farm. We have to be able to fix out own stuff. I bet we have everything you need." She smiled to herself, then ran to catch Phoenix, who was sidetracked chasing a lizard half-way to the lake.

Phoenix stopped to let Adela catch her. As she placed Phoenix back in her pen, she stared at them with golden eyes and a baleful "what did I do to be put in jail?" expression. Pulling another box from deep inside the trunk, Adela asked, "What makes her fly so fast?"

"Phoenix has the space drive genetically engineered inside her. It grows as she grows," Roger replied as he untangled a large, flexible duck-shaped harness covered with electrodes and tiny sensors. "Her food provides the calcium, copper, silicon, iron, titanium, nitrogen, all the elements she needs, to grow the little resonant metal cavity inside her chest. That hollow metal cavity is the very heart of the space drive."

Roger leaned over the wide table that was his control center, separating the duck frames he had brought. Sensors were cleverly interwoven throughout them, measuring a wide range of properties. He would need them all working for a good chance of success. "That cavity provides the thrust that makes her fly so fast. She grows the circuits that control the cavity as part of her own nervous system. To Phoenix, it's just another part of flying, which comes naturally to a duck."

He picked up one of the duck-shaped frames designed to fit snugly around Phoenix. "To handle the stress of her space drive, we designed her skeleton to be extremely flexible and strong. Her bones are interwoven with self-assembled carbon nanofibers, reinforced with metal composites. Everything keeps growing inside her until one day when she is all grown up, it's finished, and everything starts to work. But we launched Phoenix's mother before we had time to completely understand the details of how the thrust is really created."

Adela paced slowly to the end of the shop and back, absorbed in thought. "How could you grow the thruster drive inside Phoenix if you didn't know how it worked?"

Roger looked delighted. "Can't fool you, can I?" Lowering the duck-harness, he rubbed his hands together. "Would you believe we know how to build the drive unit, but not understand exactly how it works? It's true. This drive has been around for twenty years. Creating thrust without using some sort of rocket violates the known laws of physics. Therefore, almost all scientists say it cannot happen, and will not even look at it. Most say we are faking it, and refuse to review the data."

As he talked, Roger was labeling the cardboard boxes holding the different duck frames with a magic marker, and putting them in order of the testing needed. "We had to work very quietly, and there are only a few of us. There was no way we could obtain permission or get the money to build any kind of space ship using this drive; it's not supposed to work. They would shut us down in a second. And, we do not have any of the approvals for animal research; the animal rights people would go bonkers. But we knew how to make a tiny drive unit that worked. And we have two brilliant young genetic engineers who were willing to try the impossible. And most importantly of all, we have CRISPR-Cas9. CRISPR is the tool they used to insert the genes we needed into the duck eggs."

First patented in 2017, CRISPR-Cas9 is a revolutionary new genetic engineering technique that is rapidly changing the worlds of medicine and biology. Genes are often called the blueprint for life, because they tell each of your cells what to do and when to do it, such as make bone, be a muscle, have blue eyes, or grow ten feet tall with gills so you can breathe underwater. Genes are made of DNA. CRISPR-Cas9 allows us to change the DNA in the genes of a living organism in exactly the way we want, and does this much easier, faster, and cheaper than ever before.

DNA, or deoxyribonucleic acid, contains all the information that tells a living thing how it will grow up, look, and function. CRISPR-Cas9 works by locating the exact segment of DNA we seek, cutting it out, and then insert a new piece of DNA. This is called "editing" this strand of DNA. After being edited by CRISPR-Cas9, the new segment of DNA would give the organism the new properties desired. As of today (2018) CRISPR has proven it can correct numerous genetic defects in the laboratory and in test animals. In 2017 the first work began to correct genetic diseases in humans such as sickle cell anemia, which affects 5 million people worldwide.

Roger had finished connecting the first duck harness to everything except Phoenix. Triple-shielded, grounded wires led from the stiff frame to three tables covered in electronic equipment. He began testing individual sensors within the harness, one by one. "So, we decided to prove that this drive worked to the world in a way that would be useful. We absolutely could not risk human life. You see, if we don't know exactly why it works, we could build a ship that might fail in space, stranding whoever was up there. Our genetic engineers thought that designing a super-duck was the best solution. Ducks are tough, smart, easy to genetically alter, and excellent natural pilots. For sending small packages into space, which oftentimes is all we need, they would be perfect. And best of all, they reproduce all by themselves, and are essentially free."

"Roger, you're crazy." But she said it very quietly, so only she could hear, and laughed.

Roger explained exactly what they needed to do, and they wasted no time. The morning flew by; and the rest of the day turned into one of those rare, magical times where everything seemed to work.

The Electromagnetic (EM) drive is real, but highly controversial. It is reliably reported to generate thrust without using any kind of rocket, which is impossible by all currently known laws of physics.

Almost all scientists poo-poo the EM drive, saying it cannot exist, because it violates Newton's third law: For every action there is an equal and opposite reaction. The EM drive violates this law because it ejects no mass backwards to drive itself forwards (in other words, it is not a rocket). It uses only electricity, in the form of microwaves, just like in your microwave oven. They bounce back and forth inside a sealed metal cavity shaped as a tapered cylinder, normally made of copper.

The EM drive was first described by British scientist Roger Shawyer in 1999, and has been characterized under different names by several other researchers. Harold "Sonny" White currently leads a team at NASA Eagleworks investigating the EM drive. Other scientists in China and the U.S. have independently published results showing that a net thrust or torque is generated. For a 1.5 minute interview with Roger Shawyer, go to: http://www.ibtimes.co.uk/emdrive-chinese-space-agency-put-controversial-tech-onto-satellites-soon-possible-1596328

Rockets remain the only proven propulsion for human space travel. But they are far too primitive to ever be a practical means for routine human travel to other planets, or beyond. A fundamental advance in science is needed, something like the EM drive. This will require imagination, young minds that are willing to try the impossible.

Or are we so arrogant we believe we already understand all the laws that govern our Universe?

---

10 THE SCIENCE FAIR PROJECT

"So that's why you ate so much oyster shell," Adela murmured later that morning, holding Phoenix while Roger carefully strapped her into yet another harness. "Your poop was almost white with it sometimes. The salt licks in the cow pasture. The rust from that box of rusty old nails. The dirt. And anything else you could get your bill into." Adela looked up at Roger. "How can she breathe in space? There's no air, right?"

"She can only stay in space for, at most, one hour," Roger replied, testing an electrode on the harness. "Her muscles are made of a special type of protein that hold a great deal of oxygen. We copied that gene from elephant seals – they can hold their breath underwater for hours." Roger plugged the maze of wires from the harness to a control board that had oscilloscopes and computers wired to it.

Adela stopped with a USB cable in hand, poised in thought. "I thought space was super cold. Why doesn't she freeze?"

"We genetically engineered a very strong, insulating coating into her eyes and skin to protect her. Space is very cold, plus she would get really hot when she re-enters the atmosphere at high speed," he continued. "For re-entry, her feathers are made like same aerogel as the heat-shield tiles on the space shuttle. Her skin is grown by sandwiching microlayers of silicon carbide and single-wall carbon nanotubes with layers of this aerogel for thermal protection. We embedded curly silicon carbide nanowires having hooks and loops like Velcro into the surface of the nanotubes to link all the layers together. Yet the layers can still flex, and slip and slide, so they will not crack." He looked up at her and smiled. "I'm pretty proud of what we did."

Adela stared at him with her mouth open, trying to follow what he was saying. "The organic aerogel is insulation so any heat of re-entry getting past her feathers doesn't transfer into her body and cook her. The feathers and skin also effectively stop the radiation in space." He paused, smiling at Phoenix. "I'm proud of those genes. No one knows we at NASA are pioneers in genetic research. We had to keep it a secret." Phoenix returned his gaze with unblinking, intelligent golden duck eyes. They were remarkably human. "No one has found those genes in nature. At least, not yet. Her skin would probably stop a bullet."

As Adela gently told Phoenix what they were doing, they began stepping through Roger's procedures. Phoenix instinctively seemed to know what they needed, hardly protesting as they ran her through test after test. The three of them worked well as a team, with Adela often having tools and data acquisition programs ready by the time Roger needed them. The morning soon stretched into afternoon.

"Adela, I've saved the dangerous part for last. I'm starting with the smallest electrical current possible." With her help, he finished tucking Phoenix into a snug but strong, insulated metal duck frame firmly bolted into the top of a long, heavy bench. The inside of the frame was carefully padded so Phoenix would not be hurt. "Hold her while I separate these feathers, and insert the electrodes into the test points embedded in her skin. These test points extend through her skin to the outside, like little Frankenstein electrodes. Without them, I would never be able to penetrate her skin without hurting her. She will not feel a thing, I promise. I've done this plenty of times."

As the tiny electrodes mounted in the frame snapped home, Phoenix began to struggle for the first time. The frame held her securely in place, increasing her agitation. "Cooo sweetie, cooo, everything's going to be fine," Adela whispered, stroking Phoenix in her favorite places. "Cooo, baby, cooo, that's all right." Adela's soothing soon calmed her bird.

"Ready?" Roger finished his final adjustments, checking that the computer was recording every sensor. "Here goes the minimum current."

Suddenly the entire massive work bench slid forward, leaning onto its two front legs. The hind legs lifted almost a foot off the floor. Roger immediately snapped an emergency shut-off switch, and the solid bench fell back with a resounding thud. Phoenix rocked inside the cage. "Well." Roger played back the data while Adela reassured an upset Phoenix. "I've never seen such a strong response. This is one very healthy duck. We'd better check to see if the electrodes are intact."

After making certain the data and electrodes were good, Roger turned to Adela. "We need to do at least two more measurements, each with increased current. I have to determine the magnitude and linearity of the thrust generated over the widest possible range of current. Also called electricity." He looked around. "Can we put that old anvil on her table to hold it down?" The two of them were barely able to lift her great-great grandfathers' anvil onto the back of the bench.

"Phoenix isn't going to like this," Adela replied softly, continuing to placate her bird.

"Ready?" Roger closed the emergency switch after Adela stood back. Abruptly the bench shot forward, throwing the anvil behind. It took Roger only a fraction of a second to open the switch, but the bench had already slammed into an adjacent table three feet away, knocking it aside. The two rear legs were high in the air; when they fell the concrete floor shook under their feet. Dust trickled down from the ceiling.

"Roger, I don't think you'd better do that again."

Roger stared with amazement at Phoenix, then the readouts, back and forth with his mouth hanging open. He carefully checked the thick, twisted metal harness enclosing a thoroughly flustered Phoenix, then tried to open it. "I don't have a choice," he said in awe. "She bent the stainless steel of this frame, and destroyed half the sensors. I do not have any replacements for this test. Here, help me bend this door back so we can let her out."

Roger turned around to look for a crowbar, but Adela already had one in her hands. "We never had a duck generate anywhere near this much thrust before. These measurements will have to do." He played back the readings from each sensor. "Look at this. Her heart rate barely changed when I sent the electrical pulse into her. And her nervous system has the highest response of any duck we ever measured. How is this possible?"

He glanced up at Adela, a smile playing at his lips. "I can only attribute her exceptional performance to lots of exercise, and a very good diet." He stared off into space for a moment, scanned a few more readings, then looked back to Adela. "And love. There can be no doubt. This is due to you, young lady. On behalf of NASA, I sincerely thank you for raising a very healthy super-duck." Roger spread out his notebooks, calculator and computer on the largest table, and dived into his long-awaited analysis of their data.

All afternoon Roger muttered to himself as he processed his data, then double-checked his calculations, totally absorbed in his work. "So the EM standing wave does push against various oscillations in the quantum vacuum," he murmured. "Just as I thought. Has to. Who would have imagined."

Adela busied herself putting away supplies and cleaning up their mess. Occasionally she asked Roger a question, but he never heard a word, so she left him alone. Bored, she finally fell asleep in an ancient and dusty, but large and very comfortable, stuffed chair that had been hiding in the corner under a sheet for over a quarter-century. Louie tried to help by providing an independent check of Roger's results. To get a close look at Roger's papers Louie had to sit on them, but for some unknown reason Roger kept pushing him off the table.

Finally, late that afternoon, Roger put down his mechanical pencils and slowly stood. Awkwardly stretching his tall, gangling frame, he yawned widely and rubbed his eyes. As he slowly became aware of his surroundings, he found Adela regarding him. "All right, Adela, we have the missing data. More importantly, now I'm certain I understand how this non-Newtonian drive works. Are you ready to give it a go?"

"Non-Newtonian what?" she asked, tilting her head. Roger launched into a deep discussion of how Newton's laws were incomplete due to quantum effects appearing on the macro scale. When he began explaining how science really did not understand how the universe operated, Adela jumped up and waved him off, grinning. She pulled out the farm's acetylene torch and began carefully hooking up its oxygen and acetylene tanks.

Their first step was to install the big copper cylinder that would provide the thrust to drive the car. Cutting through the bottom of his trunk, Roger wanted to weld plenty of brackets to the two large I-beams that were the strongest frame members of the car. This thrust cylinder had to be very securely affixed to the car indeed. If it tore lose for any reason, they would be helpless, left stranded wherever they were.

They spent the rest of the day drilling, cutting, welding, wiring, installing and tinkering with all kinds of equipment; something Adela had done all her life, and thoroughly enjoyed. She told Roger about her recent close escapes with the bull and alligator, and later, the friendship her bull almost cost her. Roger related his adventures growing up an only child in remote locations all over the world. His parents were radio astronomers for NASA; he never spent more than two years in one spot. If there was a school close enough for him to attend, he was always labeled the class geek. Mostly friendless, he learned to amuse himself with science and engineering experiments using parts he scavenged from his parents and their co-workers.

Inside, Adela glowed with a deep-seated happiness. Who else in her class would have everything a crazy NASA scientist needed to make the world's first space drive car? No one, that's who.

As the light faded, the western Florida sky turned blood-red. Adela turned on the bright shop lights so they could continue working. *This isn't so different from fixing the milking machine,* she thought, remembering that long night. The temperature slowly dropped into the upper 40's, too cold for mosquitoes to pester them but still comfortable. Adela's mother brought the three of them a late dinner, and they worked far into the night.

Louie had spent the day prowling the shop, his exertions rewarded by a snack of two inattentive mice and a sleepy mole. But there was always room for a bit of tuna fish dinner. He alternated between watching their progress with snoozing, mostly from a perch on a thick timber far above the floor. Here, he could keep an eye on everything, with no chance of having anything fall on him.

"Roger," Adela said late that night, looking for electrical solder with drooping eyes, "This is really fun. It's the neatest thing I've ever done, even if it doesn't work." A few minutes later when Roger asked her to turn on the vacuum pump connected to the copper drive cylinder, he realized she had fallen asleep standing up. Her eyes were still open.

Roger sleep-walked her to the house where her mother was waiting to put her to bed, with fresh coffee ready for Roger. She and Roger talked for a few minutes about what Roger hoped would happen the following day, then Adela's mother woke her husband to join them. After a long talk with Adela's parents, Roger returned to the workshop.

Just after dawn the next morning, Roger glanced up to see Adela opening the barn-sized doors. Outside, the gently rolling countryside was bathed in the beautiful yellow early morning light that appears only in winter. He was buried deep in the apparatus inside his oversize trunk. "Let's see," he was muttering, scrutinizing an oscilloscope while delicately adjusting one end of the gleaming copper cylinder. "… fine tune the standing wave pattern in the dielectric of the microwave cavity using right circular polarization fed into the superconducting magnetron … the Q has to be higher than three, no, four times ten to the nine…"

"This is the latest my parents have let me sleep in years," Adela mumbled with her mouth full, holding out a plate of breakfast burritos. "Mom said to give these to you. Want to take a break?"

Roger wiped his hands on a rag and wolfed down a bite of hot burrito. "I'm on a roll. I've learned in my old age that when things are going well, don't stop." He chewed and swallowed, eyes widening as he looked up. "My, that's good!" He took another bite. "I've never tasted eggs like this. These have real flavor!"

"The only thing not grown on this farm was the burrito shell and cheese," Adela said with pride.

Roger looked around the messy workshop, the benches strewn with pieces and parts. "Adela, if you want to, you can solder that blue power cable to the vacuum coupling there in the trunk, then run the black cable under the seat and through the dashboard to the three big alternators under the hood."

She shoved the rest of the burrito into her mouth, and began stripping insulation from the ends of the wires. This year, the judges were simply not going to believe her science fair project.

11 CLIMBING TO ORBIT

That afternoon, Roger stood gazing down into the trunk, hands on hips. "It's finished. I think. Adela, if this works, we can tear out the motors in our rockets and put in this space drive. All it needs is electricity. Phoenix makes her electricity by digesting duck feed." He smiled. "Very efficiently converting food to electricity, I might add. Another little genetic modification of ours. I get the electricity we need from these lithium batteries, charged by three oversize truck alternators driven by the gasoline engine."

Adela was sitting on the floor beside the rear end of the car. "What's this pipe for?" she asked, feeling inside the short, wide pipe protruding from the bottom of the car.

"I put that on while you were asleep. The bag inside it has the tools and parts the astronauts need to fix the toilet. I've rigged up an auxiliary air-line to the back of that pipe to blow it out, into their air lock." He bent down to inspect his work. "It is crude, but was the only delivery system I could think of last night." He hunched down in the front seat, long legs sticking sideways out of the car, tapping on his notebook computer.

"Hmm. If we leave now, we should intercept the space station just above the southern Indian Ocean. It will be dark here before we return, if we wait until the next time it goes overhead." He looked up at Adela. "I really do not want to make the return flight in the dark." She nodded back soberly, the first thrill of the unknown adventure ahead strumming her nerves like the strings of a harp.

Roger climbed out and visually inspected their work. Feeling inside the trunk, he traced the various power connections leading to the massive heat sink for the drive bolted outside on the rear of the car. Crawling back in through a rear door, he probed the drive, power, and control wiring. Tightening the oxygen tank coupling and its lines were next, followed by sending dummy commands from the notebook computer through the control harness leading to the drive cylinder. Everything checked out.

"Should we go for a test drive?" Roger climbed out and paused. "Actually, this could be dangerous. You need to ask your parents first."

"No need," she said automatically, but then stood up, thinking about it. This was not an animal, where she instinctively understood any threat. Or a piece of heavy equipment, like their small bulldozer, that she was familiar with and comfortable driving. *Dangerous trip. Pass up a chance for a ride on the world's first super-duck space drive. That I helped build?* Adela thought for only an instant, shaking her head. *Not a chance. It's safe, I can feel it.* "I'm in charge here. My dad tells me so all the time. Let's go."

Adela released Phoenix from her pen, watching her closely. Phoenix seemed to have difficulty walking and paddling the last few days. Even her normally happy-sounding quack sounded forced. Adela worried that Phoenix might be entering yet another molting phase, possibly a completely unknown side-effect from all the genetic engineering. The Phoenix she so loved could be about leave her forever.

That waddle looks familiar, she thought as Phoenix approached the workshop door, but couldn't quite place it. *Well, there's nothing I can do now.* Adela and Louie hopped into the car, waiting. After a last inspection, Roger carefully closed the trunk, sealing it with the fervent hope it was airtight. Starting the engine, head cocked sideways listening for any strange noises, he backed out of the workshop. He drove down the sandy driveway until there was a long, straight section, then stopped. Switching off the engine, he turned to face Adela.

"Ready?" Roger asked.

"Ready!" replied Adela. Louie meowed anxiously. He did not like riding in cars, and really did not want to go. But he wasn't about to leave Adela now.

Roger reached under the dashboard, flicking switches and pushing several buttons. He punched numbers into the laptop computer sitting on the seat between them, wired to the space drive in the trunk. The rear end of the car started humming, just like Phoenix but louder and with a much deeper pitch. "All right. All systems go." Roger got out and inspected the car a final time, pressing hard on the windows. He opened and then carefully closed the doors and trunk, making sure their seals were seating properly. Climbing in, he examined the controls and gave the computer a final test. "Are you strapped in tight?" Roger had installed aircraft-style seat belts that were like a harness, having extra straps between the legs and two across the chest. After Adela's nod, he said, "Hold on to Louie, because here we go!" Roger slowly pushed forward an old joystick they had wired into the dashboard.

Suddenly the car was flying forward. Roger almost immediately angled its nose up, and they began ascending steeply over the treetops. The ground dropped away below them with amazing speed. Adela's stomach felt noticeably heavier as they curved skyward, pushed firmly into the backrest by their acceleration. Roger and Adela quickly looked at each other with big grins and whooped with glee, high-fiving across the big bench seat. Louie was crouched low between them, snuggled tight against Adela's left leg. His long claws were sunk deep in the thick fabric of the seat, as far as they would go, holding on for dear life. He was sincerely hoping for a short ride.

Roger banked the car to match the course the computer generated, the Earth dropping away beneath them. As it leaned over to the right, Adela looked down and gasped. The whole state of Florida was spread out below in the haze, from horizon to horizon. A range of muted colors greeted her; greens, brown, a sprinkling of small darker green lakes reflecting the afternoon sun, and puffy white clouds rolling away forever. Straight ahead, to the southeast, the light blue waters of the Atlantic Ocean twinkled away to a deep blue in the distance. "Uh, Roger," Adela said hesitantly, realizing her stomach was flip-flopping out of control. "I've never flown before." She closed her eyes as she focused on calming her stomach. "I've never been in a plane."

Roger leaned over to read her face for a moment, then straightened to resume driving. "You're fine. You are strong, healthy, and smart. You will get used to this, and quickly." He frowned at the computer screen, distracted, then started punching in new numbers. "Mind over matter. Calmness. You won't throw up. Wait until we hit free-fall, once we are in orbit. That's when we have to worry."

Roger put the car into an even steeper, nearly vertical climb. Adela felt herself grow still heavier as they ascended towards a layer of white-brownish haze that stretched out of sight in every direction. "This car is not made for high speed, so we're going to climb above the atmosphere before we really get moving," he commented. The air outside whistled louder and louder as they accelerated ever faster, then slowly became quieter as the air became thinner at higher altitude.

The car was rapidly growing cold, so Roger turned on the heater. Sluggishly Adela shook her head, still pushed down into the seat by acceleration. "I think my ears just popped. Does that mean anything?" she asked.

He frowned. "It means I forgot to turn on our air supply. Thank you," he replied, smiling at her. He reached under the seat and turned a valve. "We have just entered the stratosphere. The fact that we still have good pressure at this altitude means the car is well sealed. That's a big relief."

As they continued almost climbing almost vertically, the sky in front of them slowly changed color. Over the next few minutes it transformed from light blue to deep blue, shading darker and fainter to an even deeper blue, finally fading to black. "Hey, is that a star?" Adela asked, moving her head with an effort. Roger only smiled, busy with the computer and controls, visibly happy that everything was working well. Looking in every direction, she noticed a few faint stars starting to appear. "None of these stars are twinkling. And the whistling stopped." She looked at Roger. "Does that mean there's no air outside?"

"I should have washed the windows. But, you're right, we are now above almost all of the atmosphere. We're barely in space. We will be in LEO soon." When she looked at him quizzically, he continued. "Sorry, Low Earth Orbit. That means just above the atmosphere, like the space station. It is where most satellites live, because it is the easiest part of space to reach. Actually, there is still the tiniest bit of air there, so any satellite in LEO will eventually slow down. As they slow down they start to drop, re-enter the atmosphere, and almost always burn up before they hit the Earth."

The image of their car blazing across the sky like a meteor flashed unexpectedly through her mind. "But to answer your question, there is no air in space to make stars twinkle. That's why telescopes in space take perfect pictures every time."

Adela leaned over to read what Roger was typing into the computer. "How do you find where the space station is going to be? It's moving really fast, isn't it?"

"It is orbiting at a little over 17,000 miles an hour. That is about as slow as you can go, this close to the Earth, and not fall down into the atmosphere." He pointed at the screen. "These two long lines of numbers are the TLE's for the space station. The two lines below it are the TLE's of our current trajectory." He glanced up at her for a second. "Two Line Elements. They contain all the properties of an object orbiting around the Earth, so you can predict where it will be at any time in the future. I simply make our path intersect the orbit of the space station. We should come out right next to it." Roger checked the rows of gauges they installed on and above the dashboard, and started leveling out their climb.

12 FREE FALL

"We should be coming up on the space station in about 15 minutes. This month it passes over Florida every 92 minutes." As they circled east around the Earth, the Earth's curvature became apparent in the blue haze beneath them. Ahead was a beautiful blue ocean; deep blue to the left and right as far as the eye could see. Far ahead was brown land then blackness, as sharp as if cut by a knife. Formations of white clouds contrasted with the blues of atmosphere and ocean, filling the gaps to the distant black horizon.

Adela unstrapped and climbed into the back. Peeking out the rear windows at the disappearing eastern United States coastline, she gasped. "This is incredible!" She crawled to each window, squealing at the different views. "No one at school is going to believe this. How high are we?"

"We are currently about one hundred and sixty miles in altitude, and climbing." Roger turned briefly to watch her, then back, smiling so she could not see him. "The space station is orbiting about one hundred and seventy-five miles up, much lower than it should. OK, young lady, if you've seen enough, you need to strap back in."

They enjoyed the panorama as they journeyed on, pointing out new sights to each other. Suddenly, like the flicking of a switch, everything went from brightly lit to near-total darkness. "We just crossed the terminator, so we are in the Earth's shadow," Roger said. He turned the dash lights to their dimmest setting, so their eyes could adjust to the darkness. "Up here in LEO the night lasts about as long as the daylight, each about 45 minutes," he said to her unasked question. Although nothing changed other than entering nighttime, an unexpected silence seemed to permeate the darkness.

Adela decided the flutter in the pit of her stomach, now forcing its way into her consciousness, was simple anxiety. Like the first day of school. Even sitting next to Roger, it was lonely in the gloom. She stroked Louie, his claws still riveted deeply into the seat. He nervously returned a few of her strokes, using no more than a few short, quick thrusts of his muzzle.

Roger gazed at her, sensing her change of expression in the darkness. "Kind of quiet, isn't it? Shhh. Listen," Roger said softly. "You know what these sounds mean, you helped create them." From the rear of the car, the space drive hummed constantly, and comfortingly. Compressed air hissed softly under their seat, while the reassuring purr of the heater kept them company in front. "Brrr. Feel the chill? I insulated this car pretty well, but never intended it for space. I'm glad I installed a truck-sized heater about five years ago." Roger cranked the heat up further, bathing them with warm air. "We'll be fine."

He had thoughtfully installed two windows in the floor, furnishing a breathtaking view of the Earth below. The moon above provided the solitary source of illumination. It was only half-full, but Adela's eyes were soon dark-adapted enough to see the continents and oceans below.

Adela unstrapped her harness and knelt on the floor, face pressed close to the window. She did not notice she was blabbering as distant street-lit cities rolled leisurely by underneath. "Africa! You said that must be Africa. Right? It's so dark. And down there – what's that? That's a big city. It has to be. Is that the Indian ocean next to it? Can the ocean glow?" Louie, silent throughout the voyage, tried to give a practiced meow of feline-aloofness but ended with a choking yawn. His eyes were wide as he looked around, trying to comprehend why his stomach was feeling as if he was in the midst of a long, long jump.

"We should be there by now. I wish we had radar," Roger muttered, face close to the screen as he checked the computer again. "Can you see the station anywhere? It should be just ahead. There is plenty of moonlight to see by." Pushing herself up forcefully from the floor, Adela bounced into the ceiling. Hastily snagging one of her belts, she tried wriggling back in but found herself continuing to float in her original direction. Over the past few minutes Roger had been decreasing their acceleration, so she hadn't noticed they were now almost weightless. Until her stomach told her, in no uncertain terms, that she was falling. Louie's claws were deep in the seat cover. Louie uncomfortably surveilled their surroundings, appearing almost as distressed as a cat could possibly look.

Adela started to scan all the way around, then stopped. "Oh, I think I'm going to be sick!" She covered her mouth with both hands, trying to choke back her boiling stomach. "Geerg – Rahg - ulp, what's happening?"

Roger was swallowing noticeably, his skinny Adam's apple bobbing up and down as he turned to her. "We're weightless. We've stopped accelerating and are in a stable orbit around the Earth. Our speed cancels out the Earth's gravity and - eehg." Roger bent sideways, reaching into the dashboard. "Here, take one of these pills." He quickly swallowed two of the space sickness pills, paused, then took a third. "Take one and a half.

No, take two. The astronauts use these for free-fall sickness." Roger paused to gulp down the contents of his churning stomach. "They are designed to act fast, but not knock you out."

Adela promptly swallowed two, grimacing as she struggled to swallow them dry. She had never taken a whole pill in her life, much less without a drink to wash it down with, but now was not the time for fussiness. Roger reached behind their seat and grabbed a canvas Publix grocery bag. "You can throw up in this bag if you need to." He was breathing hard, eyes jammed shut in the battle against his nearly empty but churning stomach. "But please try not to. It would be a mess."

Snapping open her pocket knife, Adela leaned forward and held a pill against the dashboard. She quickly cut it into half along its seam, then in half again. The pieces that snapped off simply floated away, spinning, but she didn't care. As she leaned Louie's head back and stuck the piece of pill down his throat, he promptly threw up. After a lifetime with animals throwing up while giving them pills, Adela automatically dodged most of his blobby projectiles. They sailed past her head in slow motion, lazily rotating, some casually impacting and leaving dark wet circles on the ceiling.

Unbuckling, she started chasing down most of Louie's meal using the roll of paper towels Roger had wedged under their seat. A few larger, gooey balls floated in the back, bouncing slowly off the walls. Tiny rodent legs and tails protruded from them, while several smaller, muculent stripes of unidentifiable splash clung to the walls and windows. An overpowering smell of ripe mouse and tuna filled the car, gagging Adela and Roger. Louie suddenly perked up, sniffing eagerly. "Now I understand why the astronauts are in big trouble," Adela muttered. She needed all her willpower not to throw up herself.

She scraped up as much of the muck as her stomach would permit. Tying the goopy paper towels into the canvas bag, she wiped her slimy hands on her blue jeans and pulled herself down onto the seat. "Space vomit. Am I glad I didn't eat lunch," she mumbled to Roger, trying to delicately belt herself in without causing another accident. Louie had not released his death grip, claws embedded deep into the seat. He was growling deep and low in his throat, looking extremely unhappy, so she told him sharply to hush. Louie tried to be quiet, but despite his best efforts an occasional miserable whimper still escaped. "Louie, are you the first pussycat in space?" she asked. But he was too sick to reply.

Roger was checking his calculations almost continuously as the minutes crawled by. By persistent coaxing, Adela managed to get a quarter of a pill into the back of Louie's mouth. Stroking it gently down his throat, Louie painfully swallowed the dry pill, gagging with little gasps for air. Roger began to slowly accelerate, but it was not enough to hold her stomach down. They both tried to keep a sharp lookout for the space station, but it was nearly impossible to concentrate. By now Adela was drooling uncontrollably, gulping it back before the ropy tangles could float away from her mouth.

They were miserable, minutes seeming like hours, fighting to stay focused on their search. Finally, the pills began to work. Adela felt a sleepy blanket wrapping around her brain but most importantly, firmly inside her stomach. Soon she was drowsy but calm, her stomach wonderfully improved. Turning with relief back to her job as lookout, she realized with a start what actually surrounded them. In almost every direction, using eyes now well adapted to the dark, she saw blazing stars. Bright stars, dim stars, colored stars, stars all around, amazing astronomical sights she had never imagined. Fuzzy gaseous nebula resembling glowing cotton balls; thick entangled skeins of millions of stars, frozen into creamy white streams flecked with every color imaginable.

The Hubble space telescope has revolutionized our understanding of the Universe. Being far above the Earth's atmosphere, Hubble is currently the only telescope capable of resolving individual stars in another galaxy. In 2008, the Hubble took the first picture of a planet orbiting around another star, Formalhaut b. Hubble revealed that billions of stars in our galaxy alone could have other planets. Its spectrometers made the first measurements of the atmospheres of dozens of planets, finding life-giving oxygen, and carbon dioxide that might indicate plant life. Hubble confirmed that supermassive black holes, previously existing only in theory, live at the center of most galaxies.

Roger gave a big sigh of relief as the pills calmed his stomach, a smile dancing across his face. He swiveled around, enjoying the view through each window. "Wow. There is simply no substitute for this." He began pointing out simple but magnificent sights that most amateur astronomers knew. "… And over there, if you squint, you can just barely see the Orion nebula." Giving himself only a short break, he leaned over the notebook computer, punching in command after command. He started to scowl, muttering to himself. "I know I used the right TLE's. But if I'm wrong we could smack into a piece of old rocket body." Louie was still sitting in the expansive seat between Roger and Adela, eyes wide, his pill finally starting to work. Tail rigid, ears laid back in distress, his claws were still dug deeply into the sear cover. "I wonder if anybody saw us on radar. I didn't have time to file a flight plan, not that they would let us anyway. There are several countries that could send an interceptor missile and blow us to pieces."

With her stomach no longer making life miserable, Adela realized she felt like she was zooming down the world's biggest roller coaster without ever reaching the bottom. While at first this was fun, her head started to spin, disrupting the search. When she asked Roger he said cheerily, "Oh, that's just zero gravity. The fluid in the semi-circular canals of your ears isn't down at the bottom where it's supposed to be, so it's telling your brain you are falling. You need to tell your brain you are not falling. You'll get used to it, the astronauts do. Mind over matter. It works, given time."

Roger decided to accelerate straight up, away from the Earth. While it lasted, the acceleration felt heavenly to her stomach. For a few minutes, engrossed in her first close examination of the Milky Way, she forgot who she was. The sky was simply stunning.

"Adela. Where is the station?" This was the first time Roger had ever spoken to her in a sharp tone. It snapped her back to attention. But Roger was unbelted, feet up against the roof, contorting his long frame so he could reach under their seat. Tapping a small metal flashlight against a gauge, he said in a low voice, "Oh, darn." He pulled an adjustable wrench from a side pocket in his door and checked the connections to their air lines. "Adela," he said in a low voice, climbing back into his harness, "The gauge was stuck. The car must have sprung a leak. There should be well over three hours of air for two people. That's two full orbits around the Earth." He checked his watch. "We should still be on the first tank. But the second tank is almost empty, which leaves us only one left." He checked his watch again, thinking. "I'm not sure how much time we have, but it's not much. If we don't find the station in the next two minutes, we must abort."

Adela began systematically checking in every direction, first squinting through a window, next by using Roger's binoculars. Roger checked his watch more often than was needed. But the two minutes crawled by with no space station in sight. For the first time in her life, Adela started thinking she made a very bad decision by coming on this trip. Without a word, Roger started turning the car around to return to the Earth's life-giving atmosphere.

13 THE SPACE STATION!

"Roger, there's a dot." Adela pointed at the dim speck wheeling across her front windows. Roger immediately stopped and threw the joystick forward, accelerating hard towards it. Suddenly, the dot turned into a blazing twinkle.

"Better close your eyes, Adela, because we are coming out of terminator. Back into sunlight." A few seconds later, their car was brilliantly lit. Adela slowly opened her eyes. There it was! Rows of huge solar panels straddled both ends, extending outward like ungainly wings on a long flightless albatross. Roger slowed down so hard it threw them forward into their harnesses, but still they overshot the station. He continued braking, banking back around, finally pulling to at a crawl underneath. Their car seemed tiny by comparison. Roger honked the horn, but nothing happened. "Silly me," he said, "there is no air in space to carry sound, so the horn can't work."

They circled around the space station, flashing their headlights to try to get the attention of an astronaut. Adela tried to call with her cell phone, but there was no signal. They quickly drove in front of the largest window they could find. It was round and stuck out from the space station, facing straight down towards the Earth. The same thick, trapezoidal-shaped windows that lined the walls of their car circled the outside of it. The entire set-up looked like the cupola on a house. A woman was relaxing inside, snuggled against the glass, watching the Earth roll by underneath her. As they pulled slowly in front of the window her long brown hair came into sight, floating out behind her like a cloud. Without meaning to they had snuck up on her, suddenly blocking her view. She jumped and stared at the car, her mouth opened wide.

Roger and Adela waved to her and smiled up through the windows in their roof, their faces slightly green. The woman stared back in disbelief. Finally her mouth started to move, opening and closing like a fish out of water, but the rest of her remained frozen, floating in place. After a moment, she turned and in a single leap, shot out of sight. Quickly returning with a small walkie-talkie, she exaggerated talking into it, then holding it up to her ear. Adela pulled her cell phone out of her pocket and held it up to the window, shaking both it and her head. The woman then held up one finger, made a pushing-down motion with her other palm opened flat, turned, and in a single spring, vanished.

"Well, the next time we need to bring them a hot pizza," Roger said as he started to maneuver the car. "Maybe then they will invite us in." He moved to within ten feet of the station, angling the car so Adela's side windows faced the cupola.

At an average altitude of about 220 miles, the international space station experiences about 90% of the force of gravity felt on the Earth's surface. But because both it and the astronauts onboard are in continual free-fall as they orbit the Earth, the astronauts experience weightlessness. The space station really does have only two toilets, each using different vacuum hose devices for going #1 and #2. The astronauts do normally sleep in sleeping bags, as the slightest movement during sleep could cause blankets to float away. About half of all people who visit space report being pretty sick, but they normally adjust within 3 days. Many never report being sick at all, when they actually were sick, for fear of not being allowed to go back into space.

The woman reappeared shortly, pushing a man in front of her into the cupola. His mouth also fell open. Adela watched as they talked heatedly for a few seconds, the man starting to gesture wildly. After a minute the man pointed at the car and started flapping his arms and pecking with his nose. Adela turned to Roger with a frown.

Roger chuckled. "Did you know your duck paid them a visit last month?" When Adela shook her head, he continued, "This woman saw it. They thought she was crazy and tried to lock her up. Only there's no locks on the space station."

The woman pushed the man out of the way, and repeated the flapping. Adela smiled as best she could and nodded yes, making flapping motions and pointing to herself. The woman in the cupola turned to the man and tried to punch him. Adela and Roger could see the man throwing up his hands in disbelief as he ducked.

Adela laughed. "Can we go inside?" she asked. "I want to meet her."

"No, I'm afraid we don't have an airlock," Roger said. "If we open the door, we'll let all the air out. Then we can't breathe. That would not be good."

The astronaut inside the window started holding her nose with one hand, and waving the other as if she was trying to wave away a stinky smell.

"Let's get a move on." Roger rummaged under the seat until he found a notebook and big black magic marker, and started writing in big letters. He stared at his terrible scientist handwriting for a second, and ripped off the page. Handing the notebook and marker to Adela, he said, "Hurry. I'm certain your writing is better than mine. Write in big letters: OPEN AIRLOCK FOR TOOL DELIVERY."

Adela did so and held the notebook up against her window. The woman nodded vigorously, turned, and leaped out of sight.

Roger quickly circled around the station, slowing as he saw a round hatch about six feet in diameter pop open. Carefully backing up until they were only a few yards away, he pointed the trunk directly at the middle of the round entrance. "Special delivery!" Twisting around to see through the rear windows, he pushed the button that should have released a puff of air, gently propelling the bag of tools into the airlock. "Did you see anything fly toward the station?" he asked Adela. "Anything at all?"

She unstrapped and floated into the very back, pushing her face against a rear window. "No, nothing – wait, there's a candy wrapper floating by. And - eeww. That looks like frozen poop. It's a dump out here. Try again."

Roger tried, but again nothing happened. Checking the circuit leading away from the button, he quickly traced the wiring as far back into the rear of the car as he could reach. Returning to the front, he firmly pushed the button again, and again. Adela, face against the rear glass, was closely watching the space behind their car. Turning, she shook her head at Roger. He sighed. "I only had time to test it once. Well, we had best go back and tell them."

They zoomed back to the cupola, only to find it deserted. "Nobody seems to be home," Roger said anxiously as he glanced under the seat where the air gauge lived. "We can't wait." He started to wheel the car around but stopped, staring at the half-moon glowing above them. "I wish we could go for a quick drive on Shackleton crater while we're up here," he said. "The first family sedan on the moon." For once, Adela did not answer. She was thinking about Phoenix, and what might happen if she did not return. Why was she having so much trouble walking and paddling lately? And she almost seemed to be in near-constant pain. Just then, Louie growled long and low.

"Oh, who am I kidding," said Roger, looking at Louie and gulping.

"He's right. My ears just popped, which means the car is leaking air. Well, I did my best. Let's go home while we still can." Roger finished his turn, then punched the joystick all the way forward. The full acceleration slammed them back into their seat. The station immediately began dwindling in the distance as they started to shed their enormous orbital velocity.

Roger started typing with one hand, then stopped. "Adela, I need you to drive while I check the air and plot our course. Just keep the throttle nice and steady, but at full power. We need to slow down by 17,000 miles per hour before we enter the atmosphere, or we'll burn up like a meteor." Struggling against the acceleration, they unstrapped and awkwardly traded places on the wide seat. Roger nursed the joystick until they exchanged positions, then he crawled down to the floorboards. "We want to come to a stop above Florida, then drop straight down through the atmosphere. We can't use the air to slow us down like a normal space capsule, because we don't have any heat shields." Adela, focused intently on driving the space car for the first time, heard him tap the steel air gauge under their seat. He tapped gently, twice, then again, harder. "Uh-oh. That's not good."

Adela leaned forward and looked down to her right, left arm firmly anchored along the dashboard so the joystick remained locked forward. She leaned over to watch Roger fiddle with the air lines. "How much air is left?"

Checking his watch, Roger answered, "This doesn't make sense. The leak must be getting worse, so the time remaining is difficult to estimate." Laboriously fighting the acceleration, he climbed up and strapped in. Staring at their position on the computer screen, his lips moved silently. "Perhaps fifteen minutes? I can't tell. I'm going to plot the fastest course back into breathable air, but not leave us stranded thousands of miles from home over the middle of an ocean." Normally his fingers flew over the keyboard, but the acceleration caused him to fat-finger key after key.

The two minutes Roger needed to calculate their final trajectory seemed like hours. He whistled as the course with their current location appeared on the screen. "Are we ever lucky. We spent more time in orbit finding the space station than I planned. We overshot our original destination, which was western Florida, where I wanted to re-enter the atmosphere. In about two minutes we will come to a stop in space, relative to the Earth, just off the east coast of Florida. We will then descend through the atmosphere while we angle slightly to the west. That should have us landing right next to your house."

Roger had originally planned to re-enter the atmosphere in a leisurely, sightseeing descent. But this was no time for loafing. The instant they stopped, he confirmed their position using GPS. Directing Adela to point the car almost straight down, he had her accelerate to the highest speed he thought the car could tolerate. It was too fast.

As they entered the Earth's tenuous uppermost layers of air, the car, pointed at a slight angle, hit a high-speed crosswind and violently shuddered. Adela almost lost control, but instantly corrected their heading by pure reflex. Instinctively, she throttled their speed back until the car became stable.

Now at a constant speed, under no acceleration other than the Earth's gravitational field, their weight returned to practically normal. Although still a hundred miles up, the strength of the Earth's gravitation field was almost as powerful as on the Earth's surface. Although they were uncomfortably hanging down, suspended in their harnesses, Adela's zero-gravity induced dizziness finally went away. Sighing with relief, they all felt better with every passing minute, especially Louie. He was now one very hungry feline. While briefly stopped, Louie released his death grip only to quickly move and reacquire a new one within seconds. His claws were again deeply embedded into the seat, but now he was locked between Adela's legs. She held onto him with one hand whenever she could.

Because the car seemed to remain stable, Adela allowed their velocity to continue to increase. The wispy-thin upper atmosphere provided virtually no resistance as they dropped ever faster. "Well, one thing is for certain," Roger commented. "We will set a world record for the fastest car in history. Being in free-fall from a hundred miles up, I'll bet we are cruising down at a thousand miles per hour. Probably much faster."

As they streaked ever downwards, the surrounding air slowly grew thicker and began pushing back against them. Friction from the air started to slow their passage, warming the frozen exterior of the car. Scanning the gauges on the dash, Roger turned off the heater. Releasing his seat belt to reach under the seat he fell, slammed by the Earth's gravity, against the dashboard. Contorting to get his long legs out of the way, Adela saw him reach under the seat and tap the air gauge with his fingers. Roger grabbed the metal flashlight loose on the floorboards, and she heard steel tapping on steel. Focused on driving, anticipating the next cross-wind, this time she didn't want to know.

"Well," grunted Roger as he struggled back up into his harness, "It's all the way into the red. We will be completely out of air within a few minutes." He strapped himself back in. "That last jolt must have made the leak even worse. The pressure inside will soon be the same as the pressure outside, which right now is far too thin to breathe. We had best start taking some deep breaths to hyperventilate while we still have the air. Breathe slow and deep, but not enough to get dizzy."

Adela had been accelerating, but now the air outside was becoming dense enough to start slowing the car. As their tremendous speed gradually lessened, the thickening air gave rise to the same faint, high-pitched keening as on the way up. The friction from the air also made the temperature rise quickly, so Roger turned on the air conditioner.

It came on for a split-second, then died with a wheeze. At the same instant, the steady hum from the trunk stopped and the car jerked sideways. Adela tried correcting using the joystick, but nothing happened. Dead. Alarmed, Roger turned off the air conditioner. The drive re-started instantly, giving the car a jerk and straightening it, then after a few seconds, went silent again. He checked the row of gauges they had installed on the dashboard, giving a practiced tap to a tarnished steel one using the ends of his fingers. Grabbing the adjustable wrench with one hand and pushing on its wires with the other, he tapped the side of the dial gently with the steel wrench.

"Oh no," Roger muttered as the needle suddenly swung down into the red. "It was stuck. This ammeter was left over from the Apollo program, and is probably 50 years old. It has rusted. Just like the air gauge, and half the gauges and parts here. I didn't have the time or money to buy new ones, so I grabbed whatever I could find." He turned sideways to look Adela in the eye. "Our search for the space station, and using the heater, both used more power than I planned. Our batteries are dead."

14 FALLING LIKE A BRICK

The car was in free fall, completely out of control, dropping straight down toward the Earth like a brick. Outside, the wailing grew steadily louder as the atmosphere thickened, the friction slowing them further. Adela noticed the clear shellac on the leading edges of the front of the car was starting to blacken and blister. Inside, it was getting hotter by the second. "Don't you have spare batteries?" she asked, watching the Earth in front of her. Roger shook his head as he leaned over to check the air gauge again. "What about your regular car battery?"

Roger stopped and looked at her. "I by-passed the car battery to use the bank of lithium batteries in the rear. The car battery doesn't have nearly enough power for the space drive." Sweat started to run down his forehead, dripping off his nose onto the dashboard. The car was rapidly becoming an oven.

Adela thought frantically. *Power. We need more power.* She looked out the windshield, forcing herself to concentrate. Although she had to look twice to see that the Earth was growing closer, she knew it was rushing towards them at deadly speed. The Earth no longer beckoned with safety. It wanted to smash her to bits.

Then she remembered using a tractor with her father to start a big electric irrigation pump out in a field. The pump would not work using the tractor battery alone. Once they started the tractor and ran the engine at full speed, the tractor made enough electricity to start the big pump.

"If you start the engine, the car makes more power than with just the battery. Right?"

"Adela, you are a genius." Roger wiped the pools of sweat around his eyebrows, droplets falling on his glasses. "I installed three big truck alternators to charge all these lithium batteries, so the alternators will deliver lots of power. Not nearly as much as the fully charged lithium batteries, but it should be enough. But we have to run the car engine to use the alternators. There's not enough oxygen to start the car until we are below, say, about twelve thousand feet. Which is coming up fast." They had circled all the way around the Earth in the space station's orbit, overshooting their destination of Florida. Their nosedive was heading them directly into the wide Atlantic Ocean, now ballooning towards them, due east of the United States.

"We have to switch the main power cables to bypass the dead batteries and power the space drive directly from the alternators." Roger tried to uncouple his seat belt, but found he kept fumbling with it. It did not want to release him.

Adela unhooked her seat belt, tumbling forward. "Which ... cable?" As she hit the dashboard, her vision started to go black at the edges. She felt so faint for a second that she almost passed out.

"The black cable is under your seat, uh-oh. We just ran out of air. Are you dizzy?" Adela was under the dashboard, her arms already groping under the seat. She murmured an inaudible reply. "Please hurry. You have to unhook the big blue cable first. But wait – you could get electrocuted. There's still a lot of current left in those batteries. I need to do it." Roger finally released his belt, falling against the dash like Adela. He twisted around and struggled to lift his legs up over his head while reaching under the seat. A wave of blackness swept over him, leaving him motionless, too dizzy to swap the cables.

By now Adela was tracing the cables by feel, grateful she was the one who wired them in. "Pull the thick blue cable out of this bolted-down connector, right?" Her own voice sounded far-away, distant. She remembered accidentally touching a spark plug wire on her four-wheeler while it was running, a shocking and painful experience. Lungs toiling desperately for air that was almost gone, panic began to set in. She began to forget where the cables were supposed to go. *I'm going to get through this. This is meant to be.* Forcing down her rising fear at not being able to breathe, she forced herself to take deep, slow breaths of the almost nonexistent air. It was hard not to panic and gasp uncontrollably, to breathe as fast as she possibly could.

Frantically looking for any form of insulation, she found the roll of paper towels rolling loose under the dashboard as the car shuddered, out of control. Wadding up a handful, she wrapped them around the embedded blue cable next to the connector and pulled. Nothing happened. Just then the car rocked as it struck another cross-wind in the thickening air.

Adela shouted, "it's stuck!" but to her ringing ears, the words sounded like no more than a feeble wheeze. Lungs struggling to breathe air no longer there, she braced herself with her left hand and clenched the cable with her right. The muscles in both arms stood out as she twisted her body sideways, yanking as hard as she could. *Pop!* Blackness clouded her vision again. When she slid back into consciousness, she found herself involuntarily panting rapidly. By feel, unable to see under the seat, she slid the paper towels to the end of the wire to insulate the now exposed bare copper end of the thick blue cable. Squished and twisted under the dashboard, unable to see her, Roger groped around until he found Adela's hand. After handing her the bare end of the black cable from the alternators, he slowly raised his head to look out the windshield. The Earth was now very close. There was nothing but blue ocean as far as the eye could see, whitecaps beginning to sparkle in sunlight that marked the approaching dusk.

Adela guided the thick black cable into the connector gently as far as it would go, then jammed it home with all her strength. It felt like a good fit, but there was no time to check. "It's in!" she gasped from under the seat. Her voice sounded weak and tinny in her ears.

Roger had to pause for a moment half-way in his climb up into the driver's seat, panting, fighting to subdue the rising blackness. A few seconds later he finished the climb, glancing at the altimeter as he clicked a belt across his waist to keep him from falling back. "Eight thousand feet," he huffed, but the shrieking wind drowned out his words. The steering wheel was hot, the ignition key was hot, the car starting to become a furnace. He turned the key, pumping the accelerator, his lungs gasping, finally starting to have something tangible to pull on. "Seven thousand. At least the air is thick enough to be leaking back in." Nose first, the car continued to scream straight down.

The starter spun and whined. The engine sputtered, coughed, died, wheezed, then caught. Roger jiggled and stomped the accelerator until the motor was roaring, the massive V-8 engine shaking the entire car. He slapped the joystick forward, accelerator floored. "Five thousand."

Shuddering, the car began to slant the tiniest angle away from vertical, its plunge barely changed from the perpendicular dive. Trembling in every bolt, Roger raced the huge old engine up and down its powerband, eeking out any faint bit of extra energy. Howling down, their angle slowly began to inch away from plumb-bob straight down. The flat bottom of the car started to catch the air like a kite. This reduced their speed downwards, but their weight pulled them onward like a lead brick. The ocean continued swooping towards them. "Three thousand," he muttered. Knuckles white as he clutched the joystick, Roger shouted over the din, "Hold on Adela, we might have a long swim!"

The old engine delivered the performance of its lifetime, straining at the mounts, as the waves grew visibly larger. With the alternators delivering every possible erg of energy, it was still not enough to rip the car from the inexorable pull of gravity. This far away, nearly a hundred miles from shore, they had no chance of rescue in time. There was no way to call for help. And Roger knew if they even survived the impact, there was nothing in the car that would float long enough to prevent them from drowning. He watched helplessly as the altimeter continued its relentless drop toward zero, the screaming motor shaking the whole car as he desperately tried to squeeze every iota from the alternators.

Slowly, painfully indifferent to their circumstance, the car's trajectory began to flatten out. When they dropped to within ten feet of the surface, the car suddenly seemed to gain extra lift as the air compressed between the car and sea. At the last instant, screaming towards the foaming white wave tops at almost two hundred miles per hour, Adela braced herself for the inevitable impact. They leveled out less than five feet above the water, where a single, meaningless wave could reach up and slap them into a watery grave. After what felt like a lifetime of skimming through the airborne foam, they started climbing. Adela felt she could reach out and touch the spray blowing off the wave tops.

15 HOME AT LAST

Once they climbed to a comfortable height, Roger let off the accelerator and sighed loudly. The badly overheated engine gratefully subsided, its V-8 bellow dropping to a muted roar. The atmosphere outside had finally leaked back in, providing fresh air to breathe. This was an immeasurable relief to them all. Looking back over his shoulder, Roger said, "Well, that certainly was interesting." Adela smiled uncertainly while stroking Louie, the nerve-wracking events of the past hour sinking in. Without releasing his grip, Louie tried to nuzzle her back halfheartedly. His normally cat-steady aplomb was totally shattered. It would take some time to re-capture his customary cast-iron dignity.

After checking their position, Roger corrected the car's direction toward the sinking sun. Slowly increasing their speed until the air outside whistled loudly around the car, he turned to Adela.

"Adela," he said above the wind, searching her face, "Thank you so very much. You saved the space program by saving the super-duck baby. Now we can use the space drive instead of our rockets, and put it on the space station. That will keep it up in orbit forever, for the cost of electricity. Which is essentially free in space, by the way, because of solar panels."

Adela smiled and rubbed Louie where he liked it, scratching from behind his ears to dig in the thick fur on the side of his face with her fingernails. He rubbed back while keeping his claws anchored deep into the seat. "Louie found the egg," she said, so quietly he could barely hear. "I didn't even know it was there."

"And you saved our lives just now with your quick thinking." Ahead, under scattered low white clouds in the distance, the coastline of Florida was coming into view. "This space drive is as important as inventing the airplane," Roger continued, tilting back his head to look at the wide lunar crescent hanging above them. "Maybe more. You could leave in the morning for an exploring trip on the moon, and be home in time for dinner. Getting to Mars has always taken six to nine months, but now with the space drive it will be days. Humanity can finally explore, and safely colonize, the entire Solar System."

Roger looked away, tears in his eyes. Building a permanent moon colony had been his dream since he was a kid. Deep ice deposits had been discovered at its North and South poles. Using solar power, ice could provide all the food, water, and air people needed to live on the moon. "Now we can mine the asteroids, and direct the smaller rare metal-rich ones down to Earth. Or fly ice rich in organic materials to the moon or Mars, for building whatever we need. And finally harness solar-powered nanobots to build almost anything we want in space. Nanobots are most efficient in weightless conditions, and they would have unlimited solar power in space." What Roger really wanted to do was build gargantuan telescopes on the airless moon to look for habitable planets. Planets having oxygen atmospheres, and oceans of liquid water. To find definite signs of life in nearby solar systems during his lifetime – that was his ultimate dream. By making space travel dirt cheap, the super-duck space drive made his dream a reality.

Less than an hour later they were cruising through the puffy white clouds that marked the coastline of Florida, about 8,000 feet in altitude. After her initial shock turned to excitement, which did not take long, Adela babbled almost nonstop. "Could I stand the vacuum in space long enough to get into the space station? It would be all right for just a few seconds, wouldn't it? Like in the movie 2001?"

Roger only smiled, knowing Adela's imagination was running wild. "Imagine living on the space station! You could look down on everyone with a telescope and see what they were doing. They'd never know." She paused, grinning. "And think of the tomato plants you could grow. Did you hear about the prize winners my mom grew last year? Huge tomatoes because there's no gravity to pull them down. Floating basketball sized tomatoes," she giggled. "We'd put stickers on them saying 'Grown in Space.'" She turned to Roger. "I really want to live on the space station."

Adela's blathering quickly passed the time. Once over land, however, the stressed-out engine started running more and more roughly. The temperature gauge began rising again, and nothing Roger did would cool it. "Come on baby, almost home," became a common refrain as Adela and Roger took turns coaxing the overtaxed motor. As they descended over north central Florida the increased air pressure cooled the engine a little, but it still ran rough. Finally, they were landing between the barn and workshop. When Roger shut the car engine off, it chuffed and died with a dreadful, rattling wheeze, ending with a single loud misfire.

Sunset was approaching, the trees starting to cast long shadows over the house and yard. Phoenix waddled out of the shop quacking, wondering what the all the commotion was about. Adela was the first to open her door, with Louie jumping out instantly. Stopping a few feet away, he gave himself a few half-hearted licks to try to soothe his splintered dignity. Then, he followed Phoenix as she promptly waddled back into the workshop. There was food inside; he might even consider a quick bite of duck feed right now. Roger and Adela climbed out of the car slowly after Louie, dazed, and staggering slightly as they stood gratefully on terra firma.

Roger walked forward to put his hand on the hood of their battered car. "Thank you, old friend." Walking stiffly to the rear he squatted down, almost toppling over as he settled into a crouch. Adela circled the car, pulling pieces of the blistered paint off the front, then continuing to the rear. "No wonder it did not work. The entire assembly holding the repair kit has fallen off, cutting the air line. Hmmm. That's why we were losing so much air," Roger muttered, flexing the mangled air hose. "Have to put a check valve in there next time so we can't leak air."

Adela's mother appeared silently behind them and threw her arms tightly around her, concern etched deeply in her face. "Oh honey, I am so glad to see you. I saw you two fly away. I couldn't believe you really did it." She paused with her arms around her daughter. "Adela, you didn't tell us you were leaving," she said. "I didn't tell your father, or he would have worried himself sick. Are you both all right?"

Adela thought this was a rather pointless question, but did not want to hurt her mother's feelings. Unable to repress a big smile, she replied rapid fire, "We're great! Mom you would not believe what we did. We went to the space station! But the tool delivery pipe broke and we couldn't give the astronauts the repair kit they need." She looked at Roger. "Are you going again tomorrow? Can I come?"

Just then Adela's father walked up, still chewing a country ham biscuit from his interrupted Sunday dinner. "What's this? You went to the space station? Adela, I thought you were in the workshop all day working on your science project." He paused, searching her face. "At least, that's what you were supposed to be doing."

Adela and Roger looked at each other, neither speaking for a painfully long minute. Adela's mother finally piped up. "Dear, they managed to get the car working earlier this afternoon. They took it for a test flight. They are fine, no one hurt."

His gaze traveled slowly between each of the three faces, lingered on the car, then back to Adela. "Space station? Did you actually go there?" he asked incredulously.

Roger started to intervene, but her father shushed him with a powerful arm. "Adela, you know better than to run off without telling us," he continued. "What exactly happened?"

Adela looked at Roger, the car, then her mother, finally her father. She gestured at the outside of the car, the computer inside, then up at the sky.

"I'm sorry. I didn't tell you. I … It all happened so fast." The intensity of the past few hours finally crested, and she started to cry. "We got the car working, and just took off. We had to leave that minute, or we'd miss the space station." She sniffled, then continued. "Dad, the space station is about to crash into the sea. The astronauts are going to die unless we help them. We had the tools they needed to help fix it. Only we lost them on the way up and didn't know it."

"Mr. Bailey," Roger said quietly, "By saving NASA's last super-duck your daughter has saved the space station. And the manned space program. Opened the solar system for human colonization." By now Roger was gazing at the half-moon overhead in the sky, his mouth open. It suddenly seemed much closer. "Helped make the world's first space-faring car," he said even more softly. "Just think, with a flying car in every driveway, traffic jams will disappear. Orbiting solar power stations can provide all the electricity humanity needs. This could put an end to global warming, hopefully before Cape Canaveral and Florida go back underwater."

"All I care about is her safety," responded her father in a tight voice. "You could have been killed." He put his arm around and looked down at her. "Adela, you're all we've got," he said softly. "Your mother and I. Don't think we don't know what you've been doing. The bull. The alligator. This risk-taking must stop."

He held her out with both arms, searching her face. "Last night Roger told us about you." When Adela's eyes opened in surprise, he nodded. "About how gifted and determined you were. How NASA has college scholarships for kids like you. After college, working for NASA as a scientist or engineer, an astronaut, or maybe even both."

When Adela opened her mouth to reply, her father held up a pausing finger. "Yes, and we gave our permission for you to go today. In part because he could not have done it without you, and it needed to be done." Mr. Bailey turned to Roger. "Were there any problems?"

Roger thought long and hard. His mouth started to work, but nothing came out. Adela, recovering quickly, came to his rescue. "Dad, we went up to the space station. The super-duck drive worked perfectly. It was incredible, the most fun I've had in my entire life." She looked at Roger, whose face was still ashen, and laughed. "At least, no problems we couldn't fix!"

Adela's father was circling the car for a second time. "You went there and back in this?" He shook his head in disbelief. "I cannot believe you survived in this crazy thing." He walked to Adela and wrapped his arms tightly around her. "I am extremely proud of you." He smiled for the first time.

"Mr. Bailey, Adela is the most gifted engineer I've ever seen. She is a natural, particularly under pressure." Roger looked at Adela with a serious face. "Performing well under pressure is a critically important trait for astronauts. It can mean life or death, sometimes."

"Are you going back to the space station tomorrow? When can we put a super-duck drive in my dad's truck?" Adela asked. "That would be so cool. Oh – I want a little one in my four-wheeler! Are you flying back to NASA? You'll need to recharge the batteries."

Roger held up a hand, palm outward, interrupting her. "Whoa, whoa, young lady. One thing at a time." He looked for the sun, which had disappeared behind the house. The entire yard was now cast in shadow. "I need to leave, but this car is definitely in no condition to fly back to Kennedy. Or even drive. I need to work on it all night if it is going to fly back to the station tomorrow morning, but that's OK." He shook his head, smiling. "Now that the astronauts have seen us, I imagine there will be a crew waiting for me when I get back to Kennedy. Hopefully not to lock me up. At least I can put them to work. No one would believe me if I told them we flew there today."

"Can I give your car a lift back to Kennedy? It's only about a hundred miles. I have a flatbed trailer we can put it on." Adela's father motioned to the nearest barn.

But Roger was already far away, doing the math, his head tilted sideways. "Uh, yes, why, thank you very much. Yes, um, we can leave whenever you want." *To boost the 400,000 kg space station into a higher orbit quickly, he was going to need more power than he could possibly carry in his car. He had maybe three full days remaining before the station dropped to an irretrievably low altitude and started to break up. Instead, by using the 100 kilowatts generated by the stations' solar panels for power, he should be able to achieve an orbital boost of . . .*

Adela interrupted his thoughts. "Can you bring this car back for my science project?" She was looking at Roger, then at each of her parents. "No one is going to believe me until they actually see it fly."

Roger was opening his mouth to answer when they heard Louie's strange yowl echoing inside the workshop. Her nascent worry about Phoenix unexpectedly exploding, Adela ran inside, followed by the others.

Phoenix was snuggled down in her nest in the furthest corner of the workshop. As they gathered round in the dimness, Louie sprang at her gently while yowling, his special move for helping Adela gather eggs. Just like a chicken, Phoenix bounced up from the hay and flapped him away with her wings. Underneath her, laying in the nest, they could see a single large, silvery egg.

SCIENCE APPENDIXES

I. Scientific Discussion and Pictures of Selected Chapters

(Chapter 1) Picture 1, below. The first Falcon Heavy rocket by SpaceX, a few days after being raised upright at its launch site, pad 39A at Kennedy Space Center, in early January 2018. It launched successfully on Feb 6, 2018. The Falcon Heavy consists of three Falcon 9 rockets strapped together, similar to the Titan 3 rocket. The top section in the middle is the second stage, capped by the payload shroud containing the payload of Elon Musk's electric car.

Each Falcon 9 has nine Merlin 1D engines. The 27 Merlin engines in the Falcon Heavy produce a total thrust of 5,130,000 pounds at sea level. They should deliver a payload of 141,000 pounds to low Earth orbit (LEO), or about 5,000 pounds to the moon. By comparison, the massive Saturn 5 that carried all humans to the moon was the most powerful rocket in human history. It had a thrust of 7.6 million pounds, a LEO payload of 310,000 pounds, and delivered as much as 107,000 pounds to the moon. On liftoff, it shook the ground for miles around.

(Chapter 3) Picture 2. The international space station orbits 205 to 270 miles above the Earth, at a velocity of about 4.7 miles per second (17,500 miles per hour). It requires 10,000 to 20,000 pounds of propellant per year to maintain its altitude, all of which must be launched from Earth at a high cost. If the activity of our Sun increases, it becomes hotter. This warms the Earth's atmosphere, expanding it outwards into space. That in turn increases the atmospheric drag pulling on the station, so it needs even more boosting to stay up. The space station orbits so low that without boosting, it would re-enter the Earth's atmosphere within about two years, and burn up.

(Chapter 9) Picture 3. A prototype, which means experimental, electromagnetic (EM) drive. This one was built and tested in 2016 by NASA Eagleworks at Johnson Space Center in Houston, Texas. It has been measured, very carefully, to generate about one Newton (0.22 pounds) of thrust, or push, for every megawatt of electricity used. The electricity is injected inside the copper cavity as a very exactly known frequency of microwave energy, like that inside your microwave oven. While this is a very weak thrust compared to conventional chemical rockets, it is approximately the same efficiency as the ion drives used by most deep space spacecraft, and about 100 times as efficient as a solar sail.

Several theories have been proposed explaining how the EM drive produces thrust without using a rocket. In truth, no one has the faintest idea how it works. Most physicists say the EM drive cannot work at all because it violates Newton's third law. Those who believe it is real generally agree that its efficiency could be drastically improved by using superconducting magnets. However, these would be quite difficult to build. But if these superconducting cavities did actually produce the much larger thrust expected, this could allow trips to the moon in a matter of hours, and nearby planets in days.

(Chapter 9) CRISPR-Cas9 (no picture). The genetic engineering technique named CRISPR-Cas9 is already changing the future of the human race, and will become even more important in the future. Nature has used the technique known as CRISPR-Cas for millions of years. Perhaps half of all bacteria in Nature use it to protect themselves from harmful viruses. Viruses are much smaller than bacteria or cells. Once we humans figured out how well CRISPR-Cas9 worked (it works VERY well!) we figured out how to do it ourselves in the laboratory. As found in bacteria, CRISPR-Cas is a two-step self-defense mechanism to protect that cell.

CRISPR is an abbreviation for a piece of DNA that is cut from a harmful virus. DNA stands for Deoxyribonucleic Acid, and its purpose is to store the information of life. It tells life how it is supposed to grow. You could view DNA as the computer code that stores the information of life, and the cell around it as the hardware that uses this information. These pieces of DNA are stored in friendly bacteria to protect itself. When a harmful virus attacks a bacterium, or cell, the cell uses this CRISPR sequence to identify and bind to the exact matching sequence in the DNA of the invading virus. This forms the first part of the bacteria's self-defense mechanism.

The second part is done by the "Cas." Cas is a big molecule that is linked to the CRISPR, so it also binds to the invading DNA. The Cas then cuts the DNA of the harmful virus in half. This cutting destroys the harmful virus, so this forms the second part of the self-defense mechanism.

Cas9 is simply one of many types of Cas, such as Cas1, Cas2, etc, but they all do the same thing: cut DNA. "Cas" stands for "CRISPR associated genes." Chemically, the Cas genes are made of enzymes, which are very reactive, energetic molecules. So CRISPR-Cas9 is just a single big microbe, really a precision-guided weapon, patrolling inside a cell looking for bad viruses. If the DNA of the invader matches that carried by CRISPR, it latches onto the virus, then the Cas9 part cuts the DNA of that virus in half.

In the laboratory, we have modified this process for use on the living cells of plants and animals. Once the Cas cuts the DNA exactly where we want it, we then insert a new piece of DNA that gives the plant or animal the exact properties that we want.

Someday soon, unless we pass laws to prevent it, you will be able to use the CRISPR-Cas technique to make almost any living creature you want. For example, you could create the perfect designer pet of your dreams, having all the properties you ever wanted. Before this can happen, we must fully understand what every single piece of its DNA does. Scientists around the world are already working on this, but it will be many years before it is completed.

If we fully understand what every piece of human DNA does, then one day, parents could order a perfect baby. Their new baby would be as smart, good looking, athletic, as perfect as they want. They could even blend in DNA from other creatures – how fast could a person run that has leg muscles from a cheetah? Or brain cells from the smartest person alive? This would be a very expensive baby. Only the very wealthy could afford it. What would the world be like with a small group of super-smart, super-human humans? On the other hand, we can use genetic manipulation to greatly reduce, and sometimes even eliminate, disease and human suffering. CRISPR-Cas offers tremendous hope for the future, and is already changing our world. It is up to today's young people to figure out how to use it properly, and create the world they want.

(Chapter 12) Picture 4. Hubble space telescope image of the heart of our Milky Way galaxy. The region shown is roughly 26,000 light years away, near the constellation Sagittarius. This is far more densely packed with stars than the outer spiral arm where we live, and believed to have formed about 12 billion years ago. Our Sun is a recent addition, with it and our solar system formed only about 4.6 billion years ago. The Sun should continue to burn for another 5 billion years. However, the Hubble has shown us that our galaxy will collide head-on with the Andromeda galaxy, our nearest neighbor galaxy, in only 4 billion years. Will anybody be around to notice? What will people be like then, would we even have physical bodies?

(Chapter 13) Picture 5. Close-up of the space station cupola, with the protective covers for each window fully opened. The cupola always faces towards the Earth, so the astronauts have a great view. The cupola, which is Italian for "dome," was made by the European Space Agency and installed on the space station in 2010. It has 6 side windows surrounding a larger central window. The central window is the largest window ever to fly in space, at 31 inches in diameter. The cupola houses one of the space station's two robotic work stations used to manipulate the station's large, 58-foot long robotic arm, called "Canadarm2." Astronauts use the robotic arm during spacewalks, and to grapple and dock incoming cargo vehicles. Each window is actually a tough sandwich of 4 layers of thick, fused silica glass. This is strong enough to withstand micrometeorite impacts, which travel at around 7 miles per second – and sometimes much faster.

Finally, yes, there really is a commercially-built, all-electric submarine car that you can buy. Its six 48-Volt lithium-ion batteries enable it to go 75 mph on land for up to 80 miles without recharging, and cruise at a depth of 33 feet for up to 3 hours. The standard air tanks limit the time underwater for two people to only an hour, but by adding more tanks, the time underwater can be increased. This car costs only 2 million dollars! See: https://www.hammacher.com/Product/12531

II. The Two Scientific Pillars of This Story

This story is based on two new areas of technology: Rapid genetic engineering, and improved space propulsion. We do have rapid genetic engineering now, and there is no end in sight for what it can accomplish. Even make a race of superhumans who could take over the world, if we are not careful?

And there are a few smart, imaginative people working on real, no-kidding space drives, just like Mr. Scott's impulse engines. Most scientists today say this is impossible. But are there new fields of physics yet to be discovered? Could there be new physics that might say "Yes, that space drive actually should work?" Only young new physicists exploring the unknown can answer that.

i. Genetic Engineering

Genetic engineering simply means changing the formula for a living organism, either plant or animal, by altering its DNA. DNA stands for Deoxyribonucleic Acid. It is simply a molecule that is found in the cells of almost all living things. DNA carries the information that makes living things grow, and also tells them how to grow.

Actually, people have been genetically engineering the plants and animals around us for thousands of years. We do it by selectively breeding, which means growing things we like, and not growing things we don't like. That is why corn now tastes sweet and grows on cobs a foot long, instead of dry and tasteless and on cobs only an inch long, as we first found it in Nature. And why thousands of years ago we started breeding the nicer wolves, the ones who didn't try to eat us, and ended up today with dozens of breeds of good dogs. Who usually don't try to eat us.

What is different today is that now we can create new types of life in hours, making changes that used to take thousands of years. Even more importantly, we can now make changes that would be completely impossible in Nature. This is mostly because of a new technique called CRISPR-Cas9, or just CRISPR, which is a new way to genetically engineer almost any living thing. It works incredibly well, and is simple to use. It is revolutionizing the use of genetic engineering in many ways. Never before has it been so easy to genetically engineer almost any organism.

As of today (2018), CRISPR-Cas9 technology cannot yet make a duck having carbon nanotube re-enforced bones, or skin made of microlayers of silicon carbide. (I'm willing to bet we will first see this about 45 years from now, or 2063.) However, we do already use CRISPR-Cas9 to insert genes from plants or animals into other animals or plants. It is entirely realistic to grow a duck having elephant seal proteins to store oxygen – and yes, elephant seals can hold their breath underwater for hours.

"GMO" is an abbreviation for "genetically modified organism." GMO food has already entered our food supply. As an example, a company has altered the DNA of a fish called salmon, and is selling it for people to eat. They inserted DNA from other types of fish into their salmon. This has made a salmon that grows twice as fast, and is twice as large as normal salmon. Many of the plants we eat are GMO. On the wrapper of some of your food, you can read whether your cheese or corn chips were made using GMO ingredients.

There is a large controversy over whether we should grow genetically altered food, and separately, if people should eat it. First, the seeds and pollen from GMO crops have already spread into adjacent fields worldwide. They have interbred with and contaminated normal, non-GMO crops, and we do not know if this might hurt these plants in the future. Secondly, while GMO crops can be much larger and more disease resistant than non-GMO crops, we do not know if these same properties could hurt the people who eat it in the future. One concern is that harmful effects may not appear for many years, possibly not until our children's children grow up.

ii. Improved Space Propulsion

The second area of technology addressed in this story is something we do not yet have – a cheap, fast way to travel to other planets. To really colonize any place other than our Earth, we must invent a way to get there that is far better than today's primitive rockets. Over 90% of the weight of a rocket is the fuel needed just to leave the Earth's gravity. Cost and travel time must drop drastically, and become more like long-distance airplane flights today. Physics is the field of science that will make this happen.

In the last 20 years or so, several * possible * non-rocket based methods of driving a spacecraft forward have been discovered. * possible * because they all violate Newton's third law, "for every action, there is an equal and opposite reaction." This law means as the rocket burns its fuel, thus blasting the exhaust backwards, this pushes the rocket body forward in the opposite direction. These new methods push forwards without throwing out any mass backwards. They include the Mach Effect thruster, the Cannae drive, and the Electromagnetic drive (EM drive).

Theoretical studies of the EM drive, done by scientists who have tested it and believe it is real, conclude it could possibly reduce travel time to Mars from the current six to nine months, to a few days. Travel to Jupiter or Saturn could drop from years to two weeks – like a tour on a modern-day cruise ship. Let's not forget - Galileo spent the last nine years of his life imprisoned in his house for publicly saying the Earth revolved around the Sun. At that time, 400 years ago, science believed the Universe revolved around the Earth.

Advances in technology have turned the Earth from huge, taking years to travel around, to a very small place. For example, in the 1700's the travel time from England to America across the Atlantic Ocean averaged two to three months, using wind-driven ships. With the introduction of steam engines in the 1800's, this dropped steadily. The first steam-driven crossing of the Atlantic occurred in 1819 by the American hybrid sailing ship/sidewheel steamer SS Savannah, in 29 days. She used her steam engine only about one-ninth of the voyage. This engine generated a puny 90 horsepower for the entire ship − by comparison, a small passenger car today can generate 200 horsepower, or more. By 1835 the average Atlantic crossing time dropped to 17 days; by 1900, to 5.5 days. The record of 3.5 days was set in 1952; this was when commercial airplanes reduced the transit time from days to hours. In the 1950's passenger liners largely disappeared because air travel was so much faster and easier. Passenger ships were replaced by luxury cruise ships, now mostly used by people for vacation.

In 1944, during the midst of World War II, if you told any group of physicists that in 25 years men would walk on the moon, they definitely would have laughed at you. There were no physics known that could begin to do this. But we did it.

ABOUT THE AUTHOR

After earning his master's and Ph.D. degrees in the physical sciences, the author worked in industry before a sense of civic duty called him to join the U.S. Government. As a scientist, he now canvasses the world for emerging technology, and starts new research programs to make the Earth a better place to live.

Matthew Thomas

Made in the USA
Columbia, SC
27 February 2018